toto
TROUBLE

Thierry Coppée • Story and Art
Lorien • Color

PAPERCUTZ
New York

Thanks again to Valérie for her work behind the scenes.
Thanks to Théo and Julien for the recreational interludes.
Thanks to Lorien for his colors and especially for his kindness.
Thanks to Alma, Cédric, Quentin, and Théo for their lovely hens.
Thanks to Stefano Volza for his tridimensional talents.
Thanks to the Naway offices for their welcome.

To those who like to show off and who know what's lovely.

But especially,
to all the little TOTOS I've met in ten years in school.
Th. C.

To Thierry Joor for trusting in me for the Toto adventure.
To Thierry Coppée who will soon adore pink.
To the darling that I love.
L.

TOTO TROUBLE Graphic Novels Available from Papercutz

Graphic Novel #1
"Back to Crass"

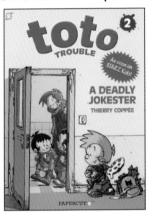

Graphic Novel #2
"A Deadly Jokester

Coming Soon!
Graphic Novel #3
"The Ace of Jokers"

TOTO TROUBLE graphic novels are available for $7.99 in paperback, and $12.99 in hardcover. Available from booksellers everywhere. You can also order online from papercutz.com. Or call 1-800-886-1223, Monday through Friday, 9 – 5 EST. MC, Visa, and AmEx accepted. To order by mail, please add $4.00 for postage and handling for first book ordered, $1.00 for each additional book, and make check payable to NBM Publishing. Send to: Papercutz, 160 Broadway, Suite 700, East Wing, New York, NY 10038.

papercutz.com

TOTO TROUBLE #2 "A Deadly Jokester"
Les Blagues de Toto, volumes 3-4, Coppée
© Éditions Delcourt, 2005-2006

Thierry Coppée – Writer & Artist
Lorien – Colorist
Joe Johnson – Translation
Tom Orzechowski – Lettering
Beth Scorzato – Production Coordinator
Michael Petranek – Editor
Jim Salicrup
Editor-in-Chief

ISBN: 978-1-62991-044-4 paperback edition
ISBN: 978-1-62991-070-3 hardcover edition

Printed in China
September 2014 by New Era Printing LTD
Unit C, 8/F, Worldwide Centre
123 Tung Chau Street, Hong Kong

Papercutz books may be purchased for business or promotional use.
For information on bulk purchases please contact Macmillan Corporate
and Premium Sales Department at (800) 221-7945 x5442.

Distributed by Macmillan
First Papercutz Printing

"A Poor Example"

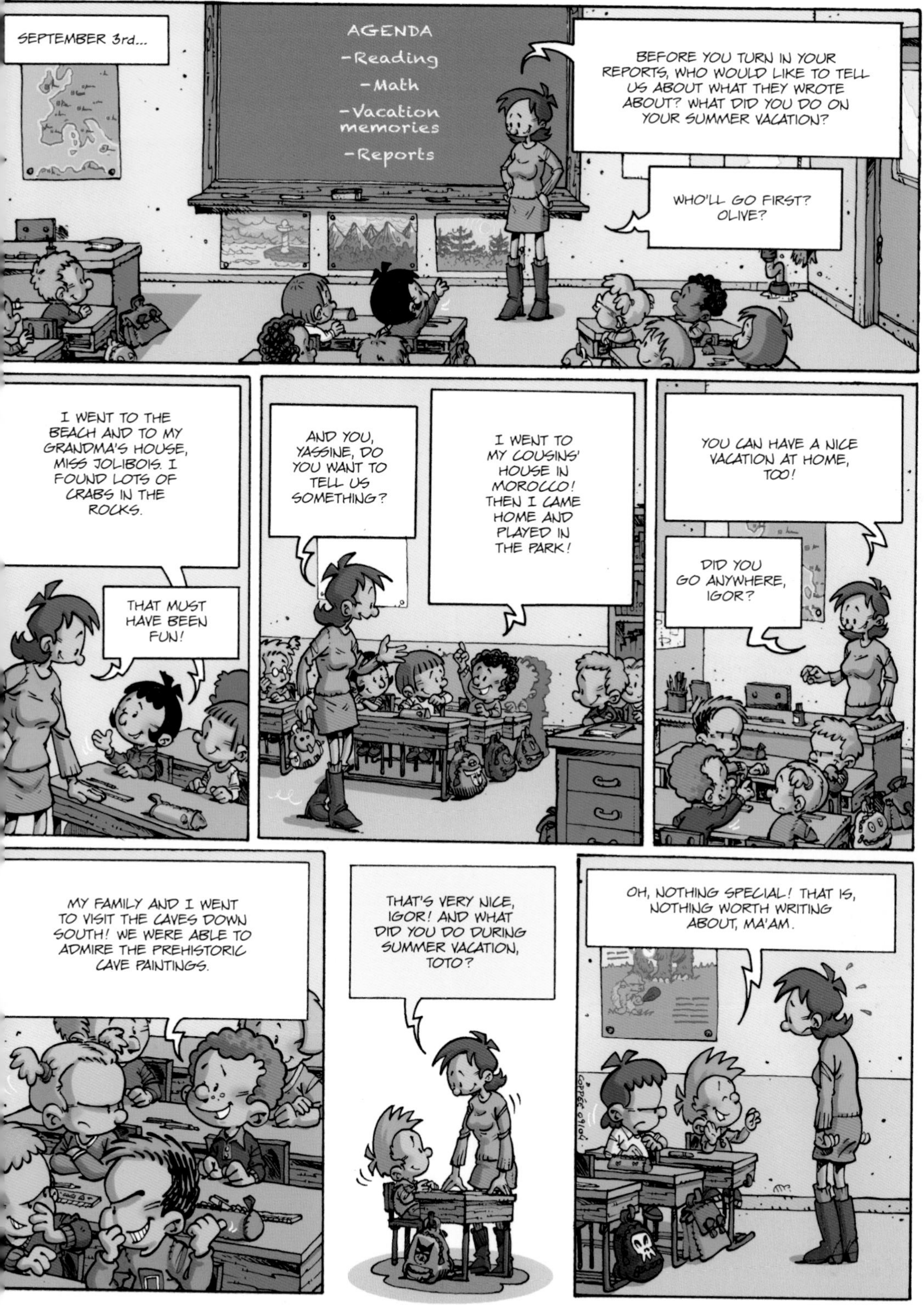
SEPTEMBER 3rd...
AGENDA
-Reading
-Math
-Vacation memories
-Reports
BEFORE YOU TURN IN YOUR REPORTS, WHO WOULD LIKE TO TELL US ABOUT WHAT THEY WROTE ABOUT? WHAT DID YOU DO ON YOUR SUMMER VACATION?
WHO'LL GO FIRST? OLIVE?
I WENT TO THE BEACH AND TO MY GRANDMA'S HOUSE, MISS JOLIBOIS. I FOUND LOTS OF CRABS IN THE ROCKS.
THAT MUST HAVE BEEN FUN!
AND YOU, YASSINE, DO YOU WANT TO TELL US SOMETHING?
I WENT TO MY COUSINS' HOUSE IN MOROCCO! THEN I CAME HOME AND PLAYED IN THE PARK!
YOU CAN HAVE A NICE VACATION AT HOME, TOO!
DID YOU GO ANYWHERE, IGOR?
MY FAMILY AND I WENT TO VISIT THE CAVES DOWN SOUTH! WE WERE ABLE TO ADMIRE THE PREHISTORIC CAVE PAINTINGS.
THAT'S VERY NICE, IGOR! AND WHAT DID YOU DO DURING SUMMER VACATION, TOTO?
OH, NOTHING SPECIAL! THAT IS, NOTHING WORTH WRITING ABOUT, MA'AM.

"Let Sleeping Totos Lie"

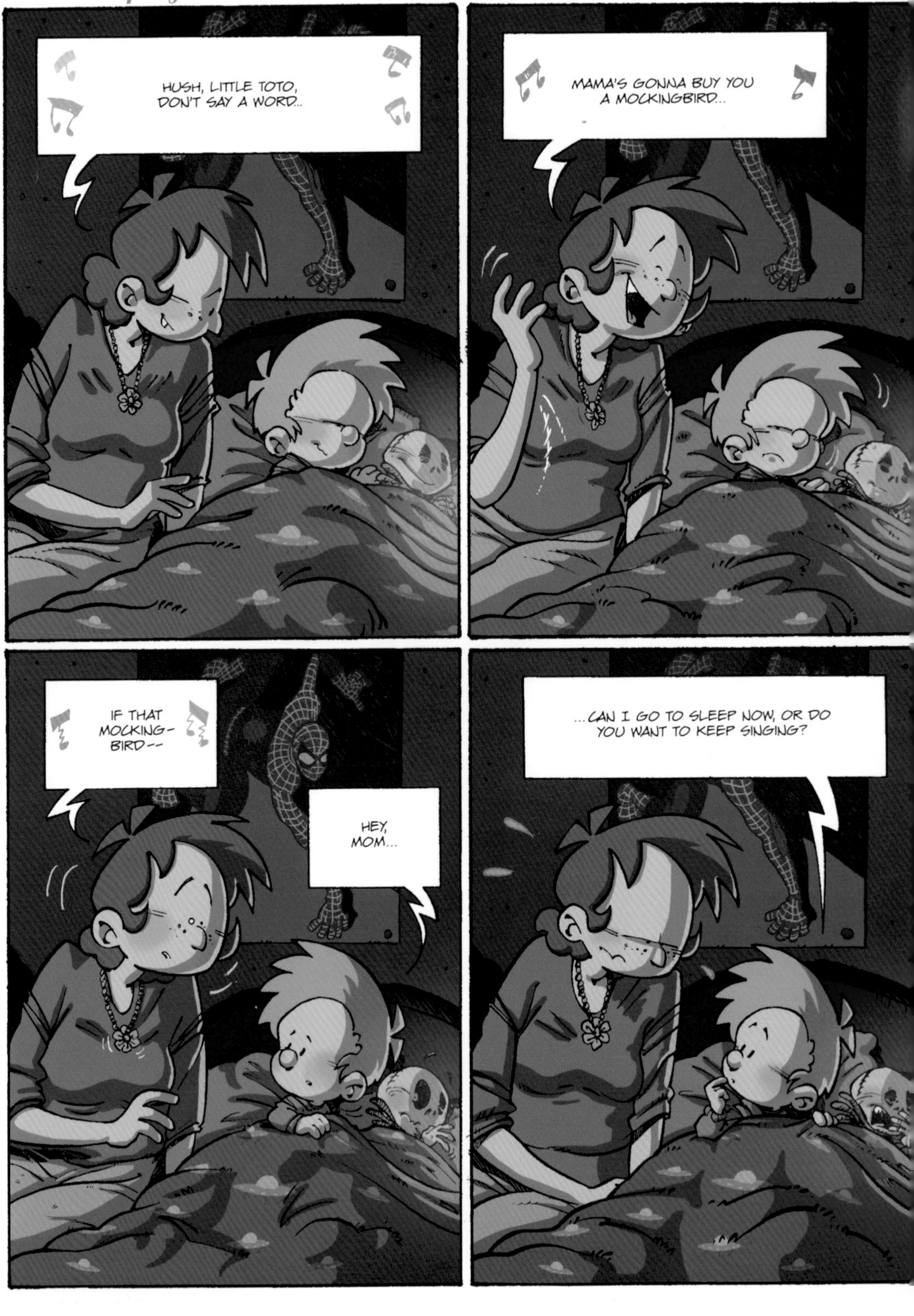
HUSH, LITTLE TOTO, DON'T SAY A WORD...
MAMA'S GONNA BUY YOU A MOCKINGBIRD...
IF THAT MOCKING-BIRD--
HEY, MOM...
...CAN I GO TO SLEEP NOW, OR DO YOU WANT TO KEEP SINGING?

"Staggered Fall"

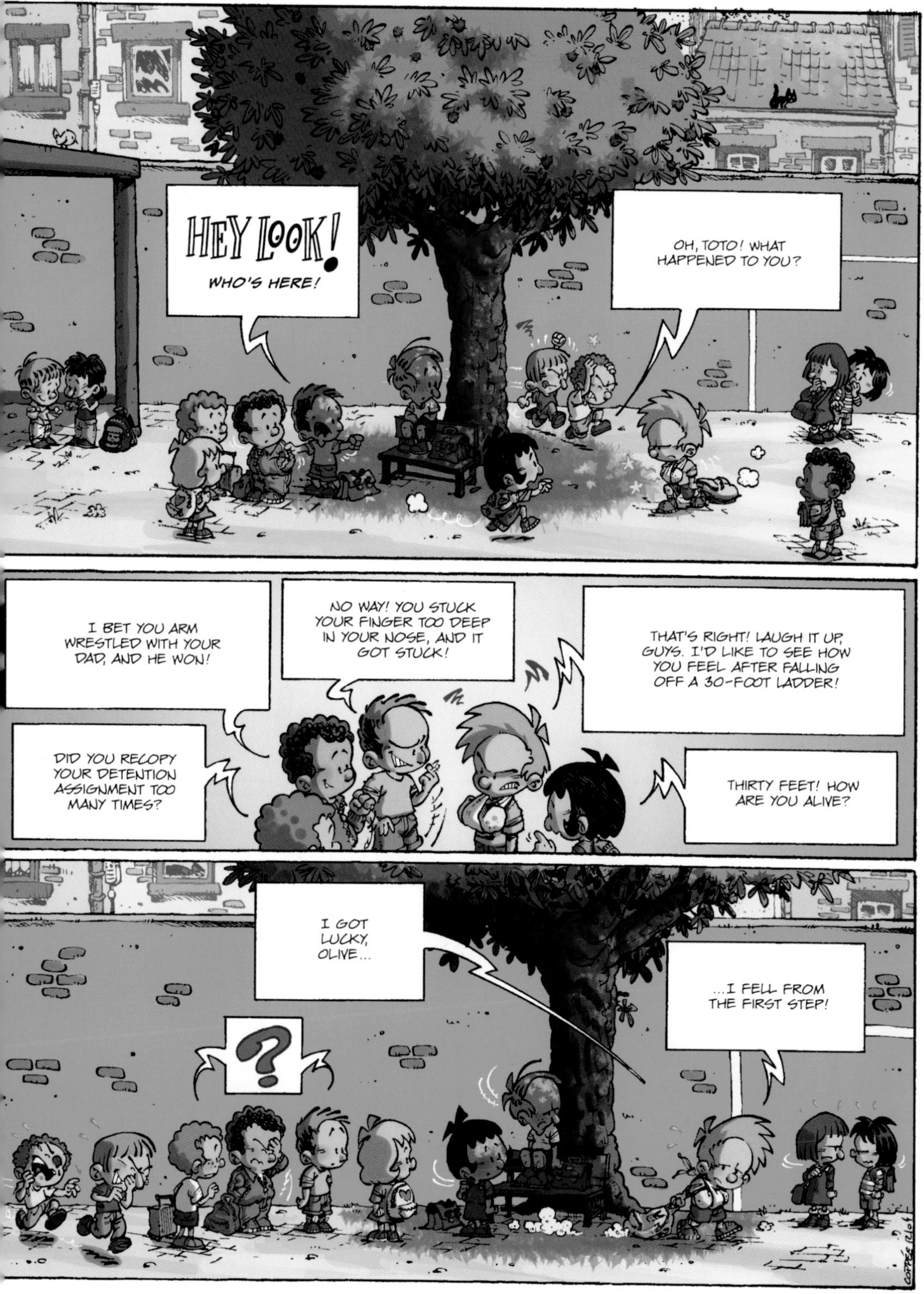
HEY LOOK!
WHO'S HERE!
OH, TOTO! WHAT HAPPENED TO YOU?
I BET YOU ARM WRESTLED WITH YOUR DAD, AND HE WON!
DID YOU RECOPY YOUR DETENTION ASSIGNMENT TOO MANY TIMES?
NO WAY! YOU STUCK YOUR FINGER TOO DEEP IN YOUR NOSE, AND IT GOT STUCK!
THAT'S RIGHT! LAUGH IT UP, GUYS. I'D LIKE TO SEE HOW YOU FEEL AFTER FALLING OFF A 30-FOOT LADDER!
THIRTY FEET! HOW ARE YOU ALIVE?
I GOT LUCKY, OLIVE...
?
...I FELL FROM THE FIRST STEP!

"You, He, She, or What About Me"

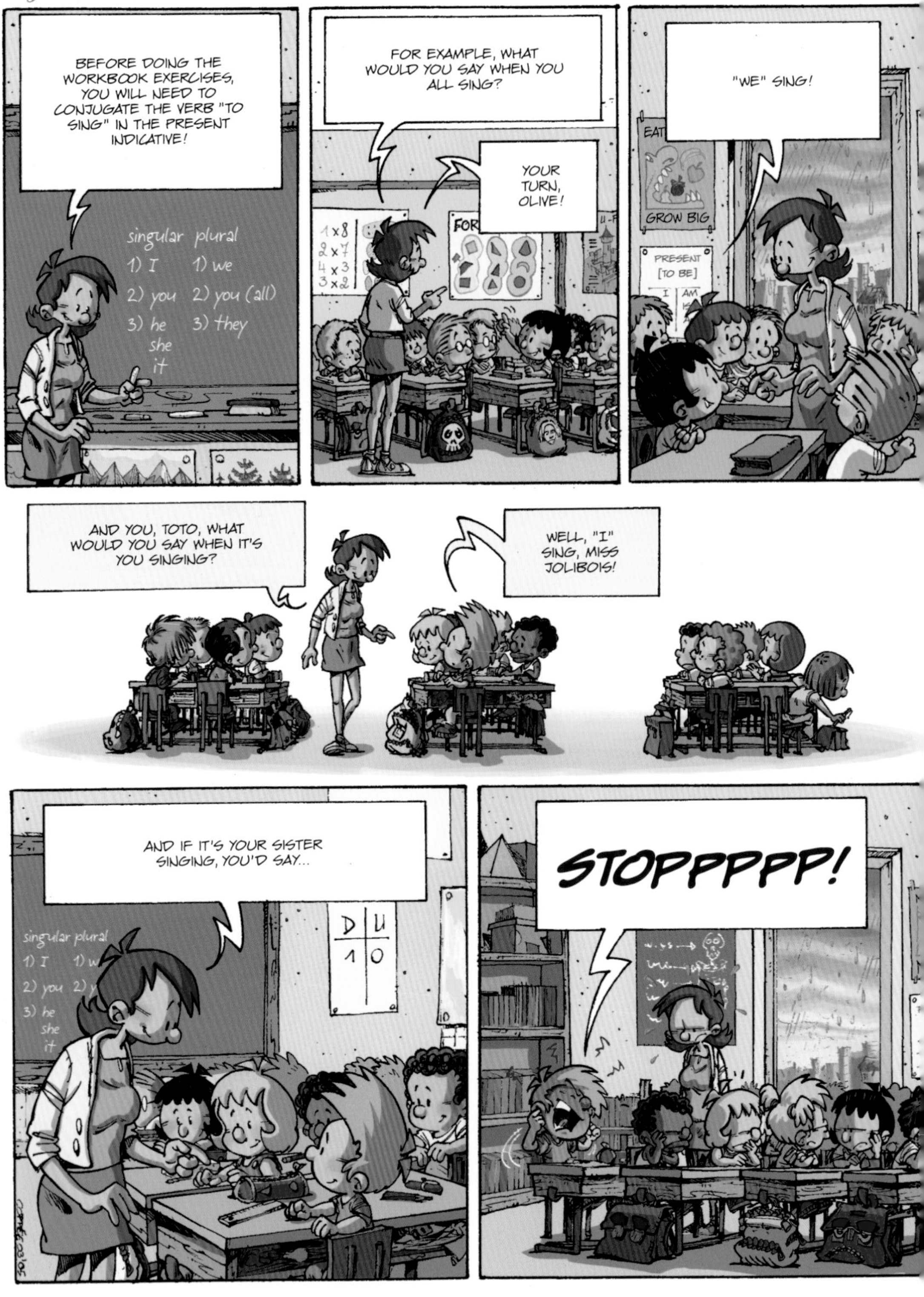
BEFORE DOING THE WORKBOOK EXERCISES, YOU WILL NEED TO CONJUGATE THE VERB "TO SING" IN THE PRESENT INDICATIVE!
singular plural
1) I 1) we
2) you 2) you (all)
3) he she it 3) they
FOR EXAMPLE, WHAT WOULD YOU SAY WHEN YOU ALL SING?
YOUR TURN, OLIVE!
"WE" SING!
GROW BIG
PRESENT [TO BE]
AND YOU, TOTO, WHAT WOULD YOU SAY WHEN IT'S YOU SINGING?
WELL, "I" SING, MISS JOLIBOIS!
AND IF IT'S YOUR SISTER SINGING, YOU'D SAY...
STOPPPPPP!

'Stepping in Time''

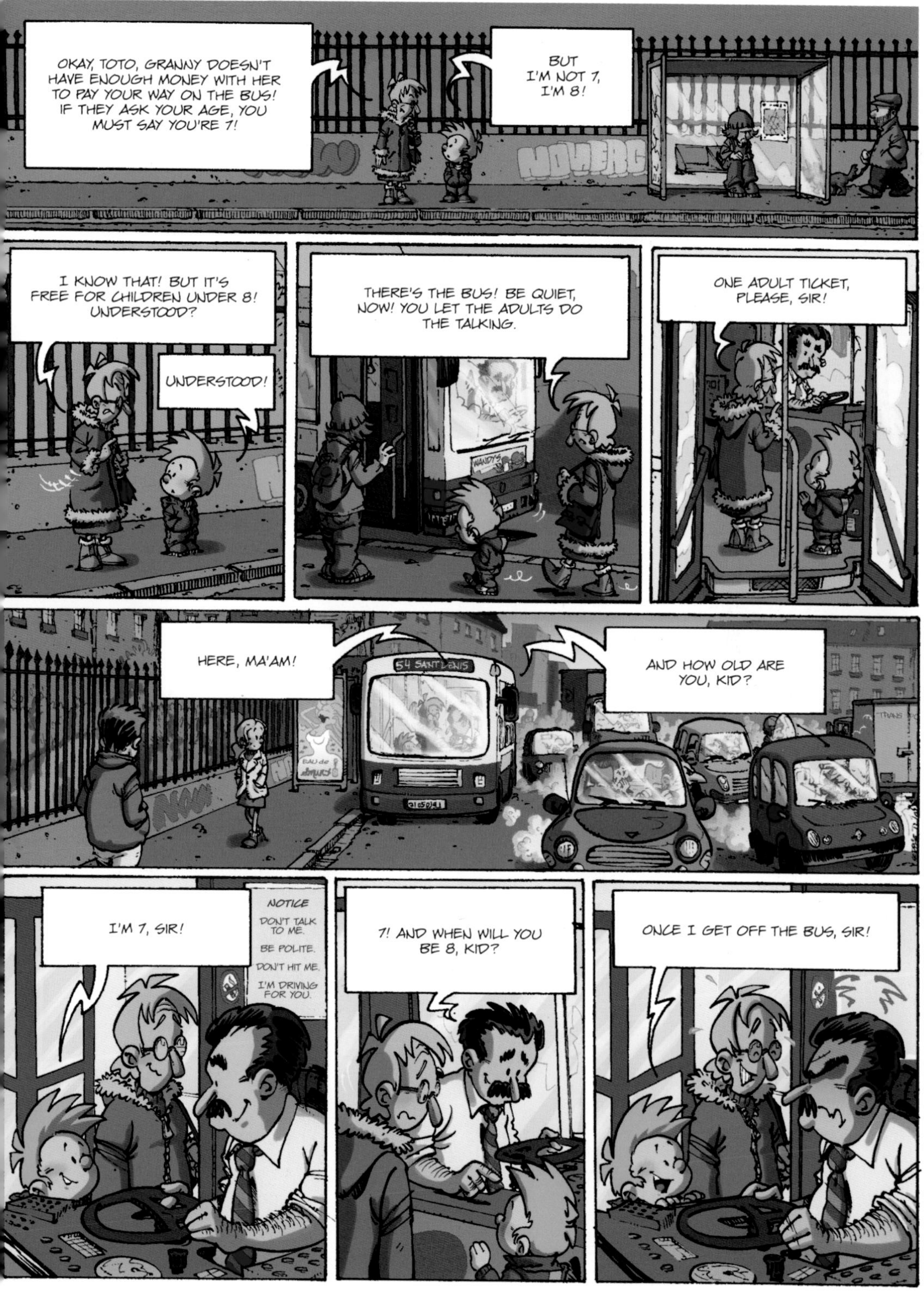

OKAY, TOTO, GRANNY DOESN'T HAVE ENOUGH MONEY WITH HER TO PAY YOUR WAY ON THE BUS! IF THEY ASK YOUR AGE, YOU MUST SAY YOU'RE 7!
BUT I'M NOT 7, I'M 8!
I KNOW THAT! BUT IT'S FREE FOR CHILDREN UNDER 8! UNDERSTOOD?
UNDERSTOOD!
THERE'S THE BUS! BE QUIET, NOW! YOU LET THE ADULTS DO THE TALKING.
ONE ADULT TICKET, PLEASE, SIR!
HERE, MA'AM!
AND HOW OLD ARE YOU, KID?
I'M 7, SIR!
NOTICE
DON'T TALK TO ME.
BE POLITE.
DON'T HIT ME.
I'M DRIVING FOR YOU.
7! AND WHEN WILL YOU BE 8, KID?
ONCE I GET OFF THE BUS, SIR!

"A Third Helping?"

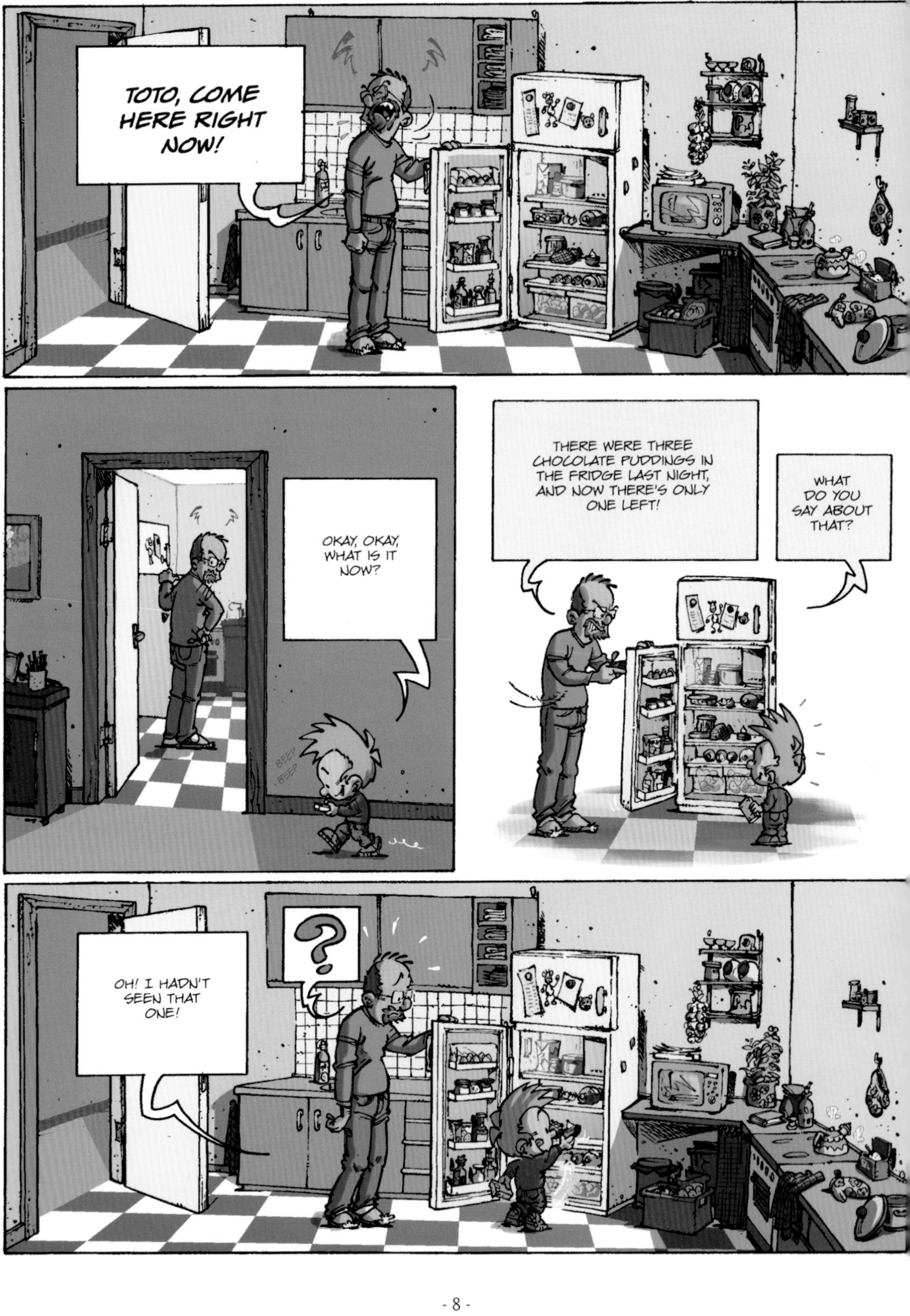

TOTO, COME HERE RIGHT NOW!
OKAY, OKAY, WHAT IS IT NOW?
BEEP BEEP
THERE WERE THREE CHOCOLATE PUDDINGS IN THE FRIDGE LAST NIGHT, AND NOW THERE'S ONLY ONE LEFT!
WHAT DO YOU SAY ABOUT THAT?
OH! I HADN'T SEEN THAT ONE!

"*Excused Absence*"

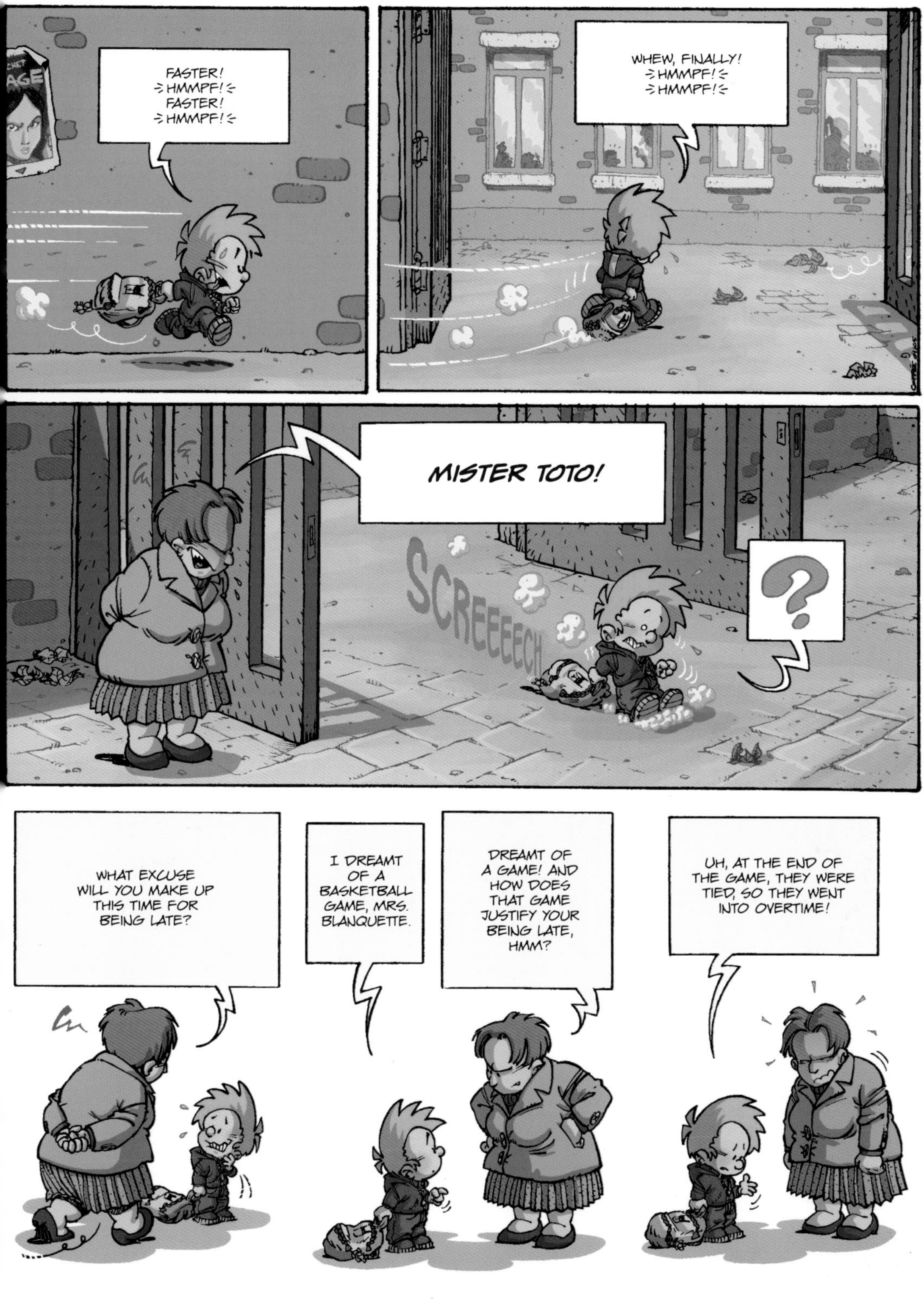
FASTER!
=HMMPF!=
FASTER!
=HMMPF!=
WHEW, FINALLY!
=HMMPF!=
=HMMPF!=
MISTER TOTO!
SCREEEECH
?
WHAT EXCUSE WILL YOU MAKE UP THIS TIME FOR BEING LATE?
I DREAMT OF A BASKETBALL GAME, MRS. BLANQUETTE.
DREAMT OF A GAME! AND HOW DOES THAT GAME JUSTIFY YOUR BEING LATE, HMM?
UH, AT THE END OF THE GAME, THEY WERE TIED, SO THEY WENT INTO OVERTIME!

"And Yet it's so True!"

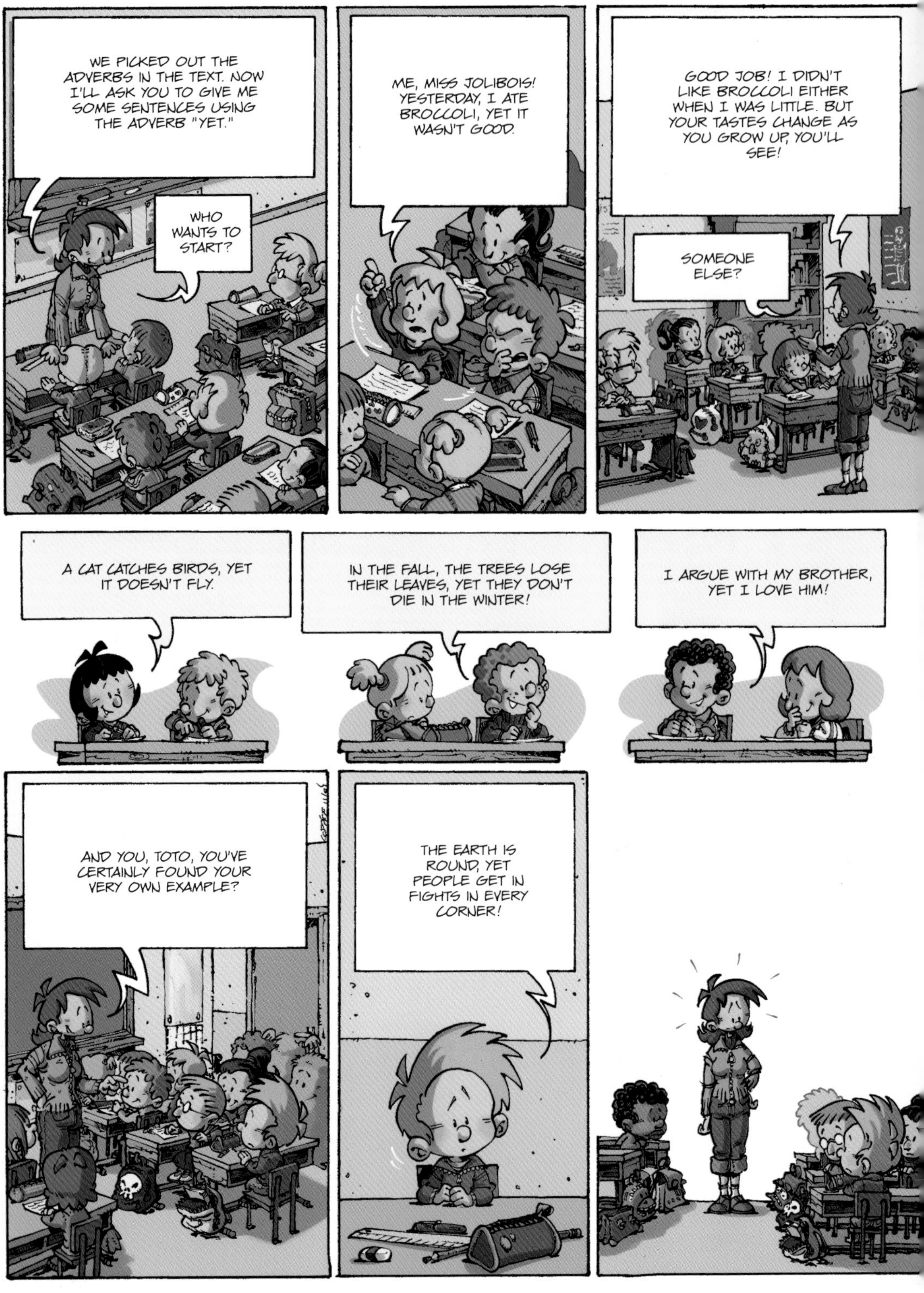

WE PICKED OUT THE ADVERBS IN THE TEXT. NOW I'LL ASK YOU TO GIVE ME SOME SENTENCES USING THE ADVERB "YET."
WHO WANTS TO START?
ME, MISS JOLIBOIS! YESTERDAY, I ATE BROCCOLI, YET IT WASN'T GOOD.
GOOD JOB! I DIDN'T LIKE BROCCOLI EITHER WHEN I WAS LITTLE. BUT YOUR TASTES CHANGE AS YOU GROW UP, YOU'LL SEE!
SOMEONE ELSE?
A CAT CATCHES BIRDS, YET IT DOESN'T FLY.
IN THE FALL, THE TREES LOSE THEIR LEAVES, YET THEY DON'T DIE IN THE WINTER!
I ARGUE WITH MY BROTHER, YET I LOVE HIM!
AND YOU, TOTO, YOU'VE CERTAINLY FOUND YOUR VERY OWN EXAMPLE?
THE EARTH IS ROUND, YET PEOPLE GET IN FIGHTS IN EVERY CORNER!

"Divine Progress"

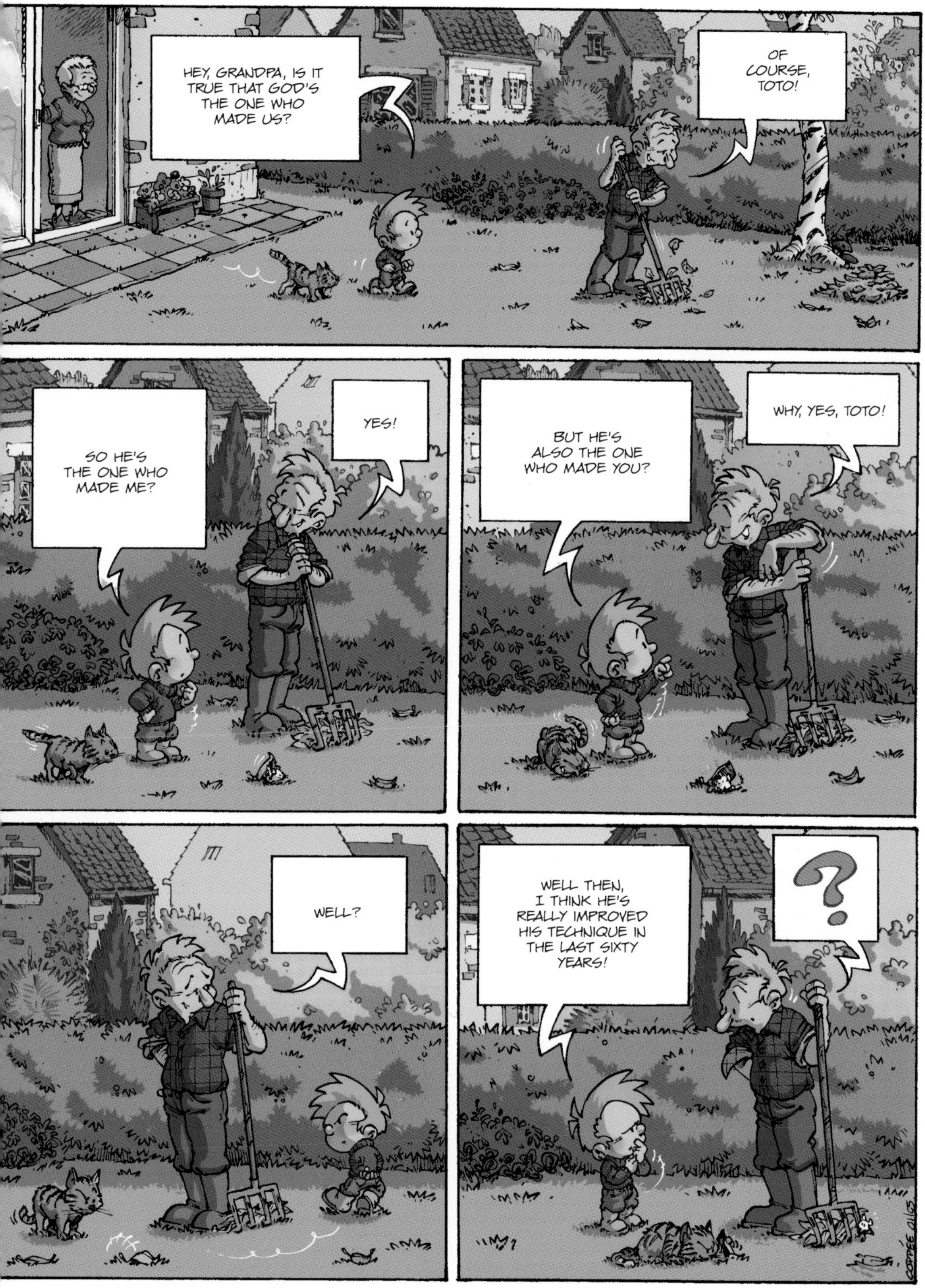

HEY, GRANDPA, IS IT TRUE THAT GOD'S THE ONE WHO MADE US?
OF COURSE, TOTO!
SO HE'S THE ONE WHO MADE ME?
YES!
BUT HE'S ALSO THE ONE WHO MADE YOU?
WHY, YES, TOTO!
WELL?
WELL THEN, I THINK HE'S REALLY IMPROVED HIS TECHNIQUE IN THE LAST SIXTY YEARS!
?

"Good Day, Goodnight"

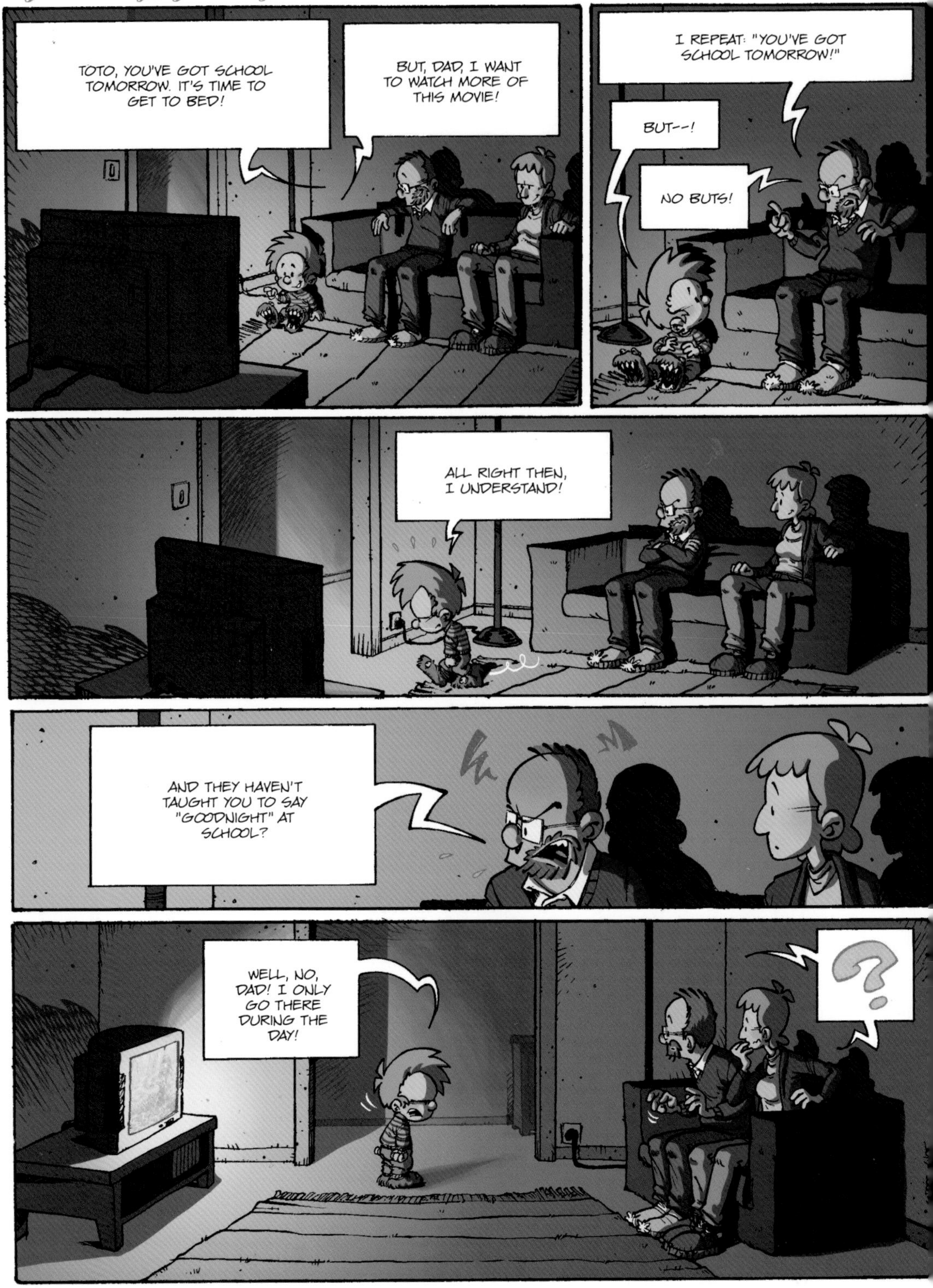
TOTO, YOU'VE GOT SCHOOL TOMORROW. IT'S TIME TO GET TO BED!
BUT, DAD, I WANT TO WATCH MORE OF THIS MOVIE!
I REPEAT: "YOU'VE GOT SCHOOL TOMORROW!"
BUT--!
NO BUTS!
ALL RIGHT THEN, I UNDERSTAND!
AND THEY HAVEN'T TAUGHT YOU TO SAY "GOODNIGHT" AT SCHOOL?
WELL, NO, DAD! I ONLY GO THERE DURING THE DAY!
?

"Walking in the Rain"

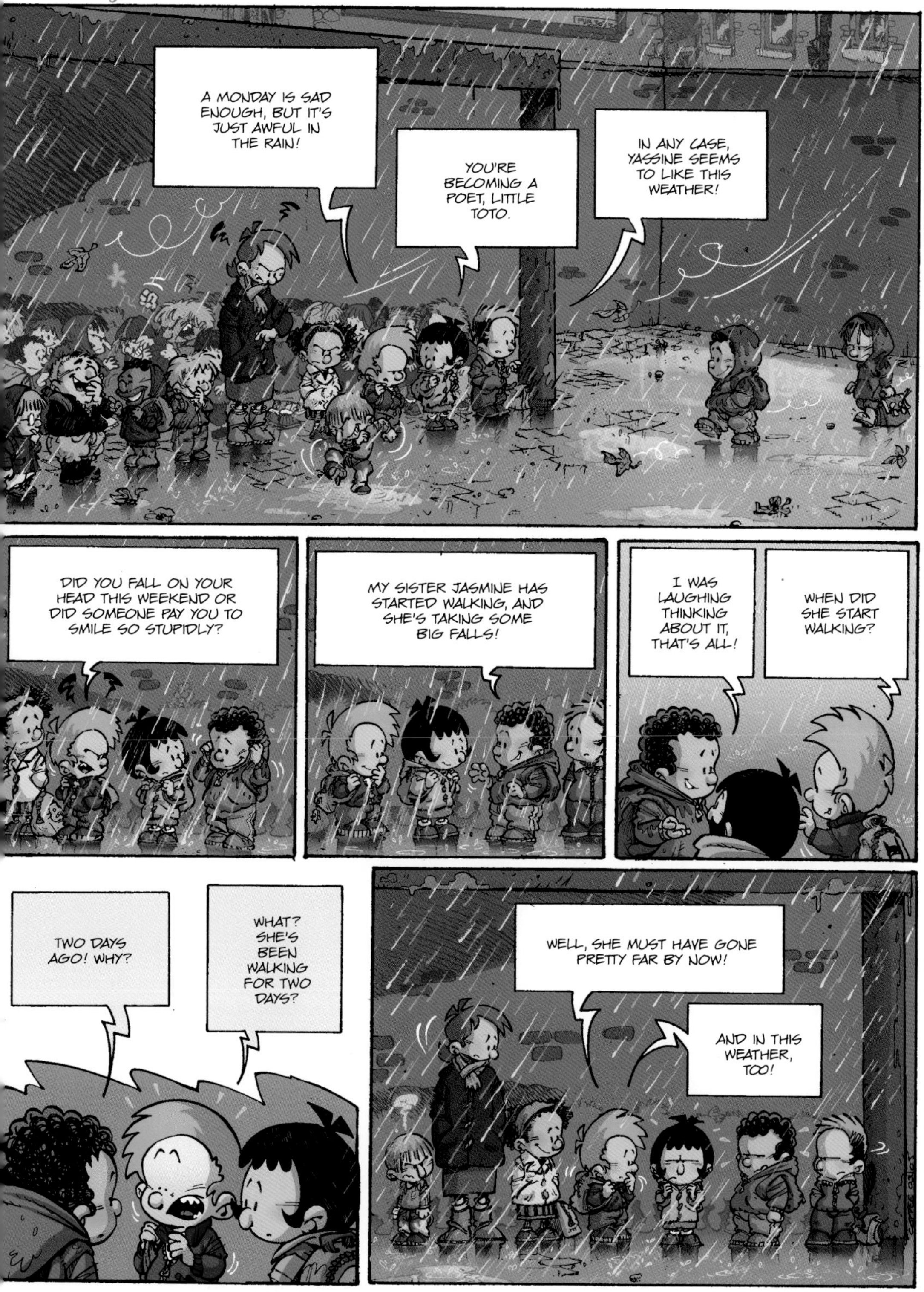
A MONDAY IS SAD ENOUGH, BUT IT'S JUST AWFUL IN THE RAIN!
YOU'RE BECOMING A POET, LITTLE TOTO.
IN ANY CASE, YASSINE SEEMS TO LIKE THIS WEATHER!
DID YOU FALL ON YOUR HEAD THIS WEEKEND OR DID SOMEONE PAY YOU TO SMILE SO STUPIDLY?
MY SISTER JASMINE HAS STARTED WALKING, AND SHE'S TAKING SOME BIG FALLS!
I WAS LAUGHING THINKING ABOUT IT, THAT'S ALL!
WHEN DID SHE START WALKING?
TWO DAYS AGO! WHY?
WHAT? SHE'S BEEN WALKING FOR TWO DAYS?
WELL, SHE MUST HAVE GONE PRETTY FAR BY NOW!
AND IN THIS WEATHER, TOO!

"Whoever Seeks Shall Find, Daddy"

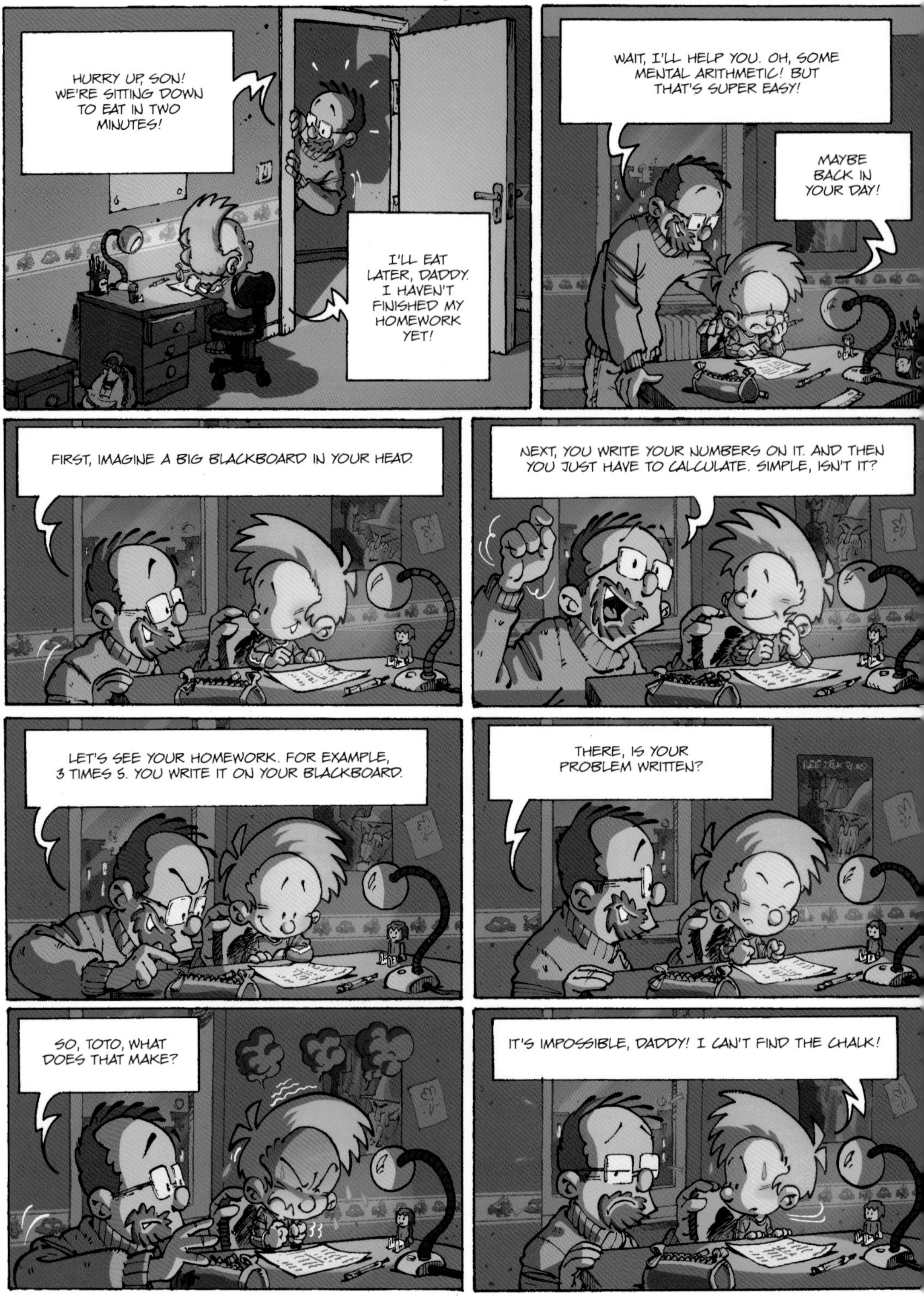
HURRY UP, SON! WE'RE SITTING DOWN TO EAT IN TWO MINUTES!
I'LL EAT LATER, DADDY. I HAVEN'T FINISHED MY HOMEWORK YET!
WAIT, I'LL HELP YOU. OH, SOME MENTAL ARITHMETIC! BUT THAT'S SUPER EASY!
MAYBE BACK IN YOUR DAY!
FIRST, IMAGINE A BIG BLACKBOARD IN YOUR HEAD.
NEXT, YOU WRITE YOUR NUMBERS ON IT. AND THEN YOU JUST HAVE TO CALCULATE. SIMPLE, ISN'T IT?
LET'S SEE YOUR HOMEWORK. FOR EXAMPLE, 3 TIMES 5. YOU WRITE IT ON YOUR BLACKBOARD.
THERE, IS YOUR PROBLEM WRITTEN?
SO, TOTO, WHAT DOES THAT MAKE?
IT'S IMPOSSIBLE, DADDY! I CAN'T FIND THE CHALK!

"Not Done, Not Caught"

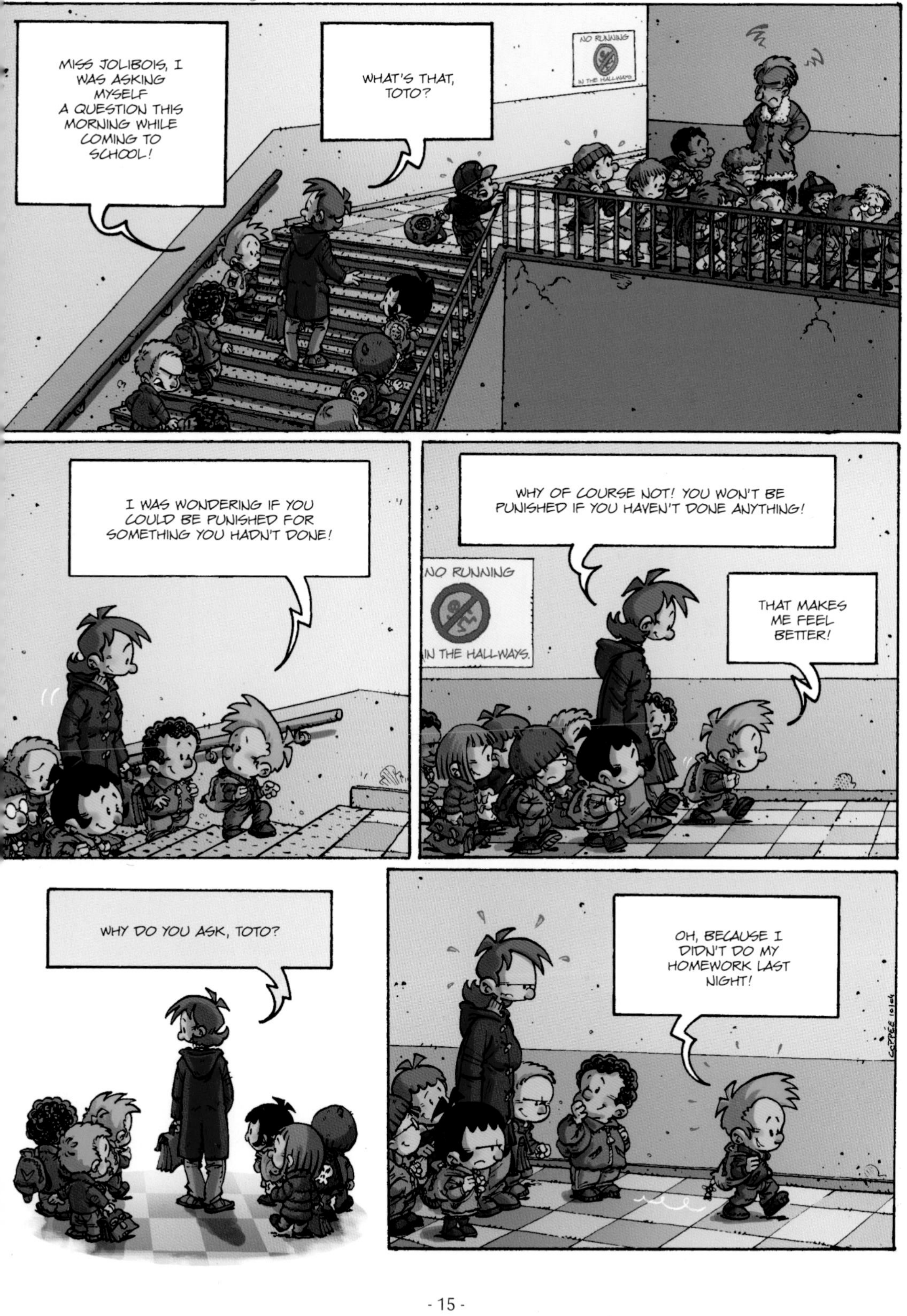

MISS JOLIBOIS, I WAS ASKING MYSELF A QUESTION THIS MORNING WHILE COMING TO SCHOOL!
WHAT'S THAT, TOTO?
NO RUNNING IN THE HALLWAYS
I WAS WONDERING IF YOU COULD BE PUNISHED FOR SOMETHING YOU HADN'T DONE!
WHY OF COURSE NOT! YOU WON'T BE PUNISHED IF YOU HAVEN'T DONE ANYTHING!
NO RUNNING IN THE HALLWAYS.
THAT MAKES ME FEEL BETTER!
WHY DO YOU ASK, TOTO?
OH, BECAUSE I DIDN'T DO MY HOMEWORK LAST NIGHT!

"You're Agway?"

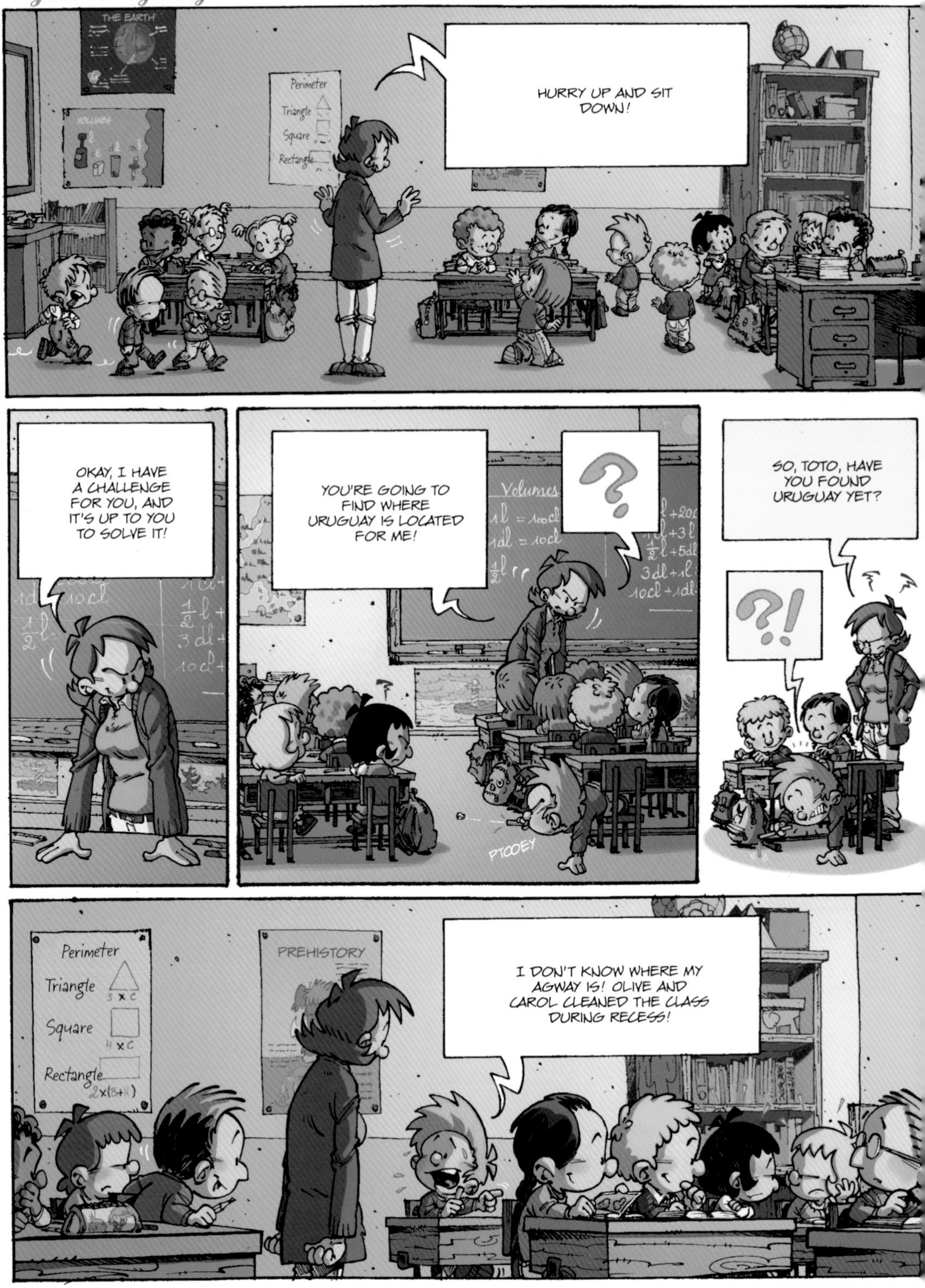
THE EARTH
Perimeter
Triangle
Square
Rectangle
HURRY UP AND SIT DOWN!
OKAY, I HAVE A CHALLENGE FOR YOU, AND IT'S UP TO YOU TO SOLVE IT!
YOU'RE GOING TO FIND WHERE URUGUAY IS LOCATED FOR ME!
Volumes
?
PTOOEY
SO, TOTO, HAVE YOU FOUND URUGUAY YET?
?!
Perimeter
Triangle
3 x C
Square
4 x C
Rectangle
PREHISTORY
I DON'T KNOW WHERE MY AGWAY IS! OLIVE AND CAROL CLEANED THE CLASS DURING RECESS!

"You're No Gift!"

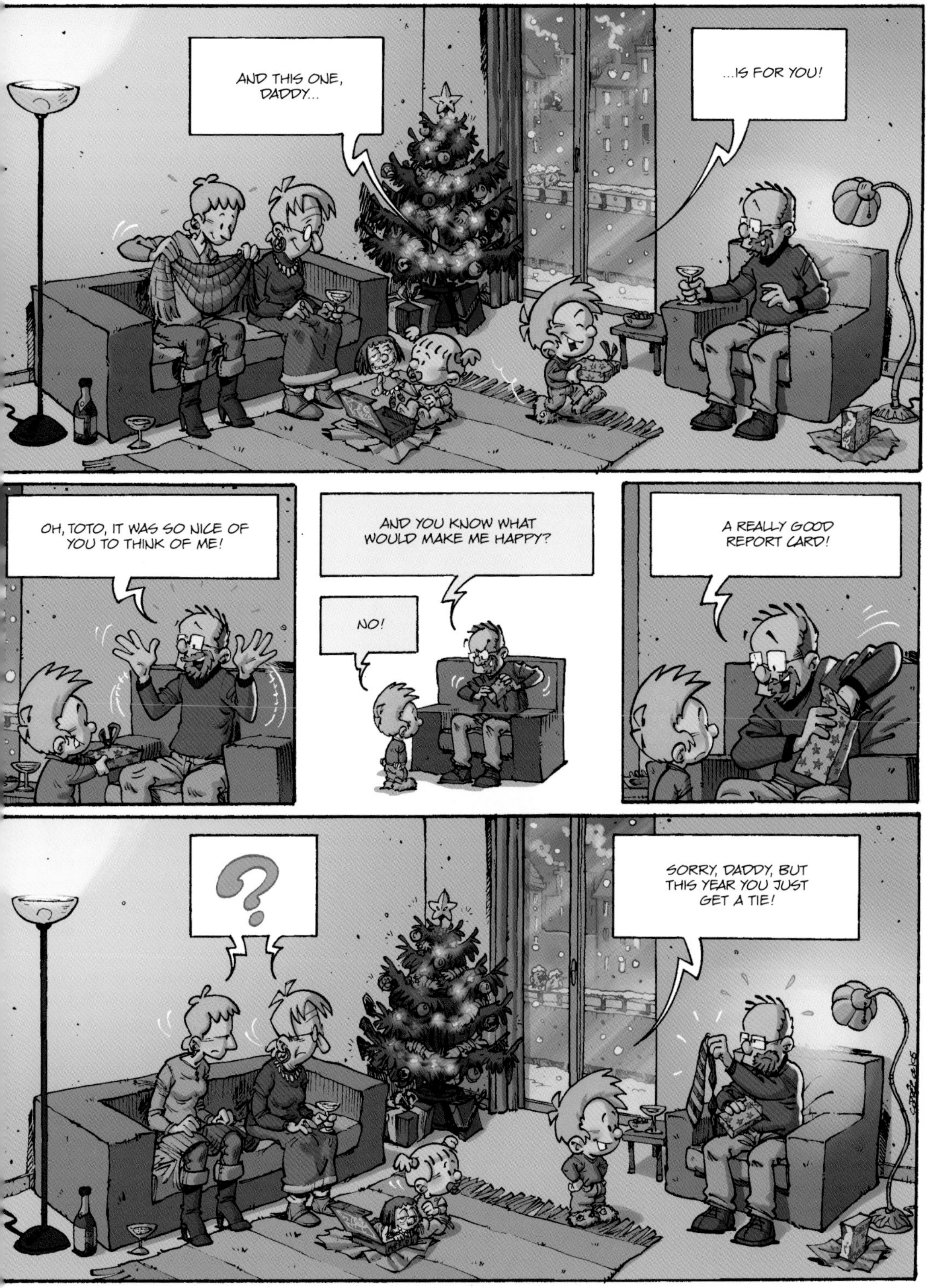
AND THIS ONE, DADDY...
...IS FOR YOU!
OH, TOTO, IT WAS SO NICE OF YOU TO THINK OF ME!
AND YOU KNOW WHAT WOULD MAKE ME HAPPY?
NO!
A REALLY GOOD REPORT CARD!
?
SORRY, DADDY, BUT THIS YEAR YOU JUST GET A TIE!

"The Truth Hurts"

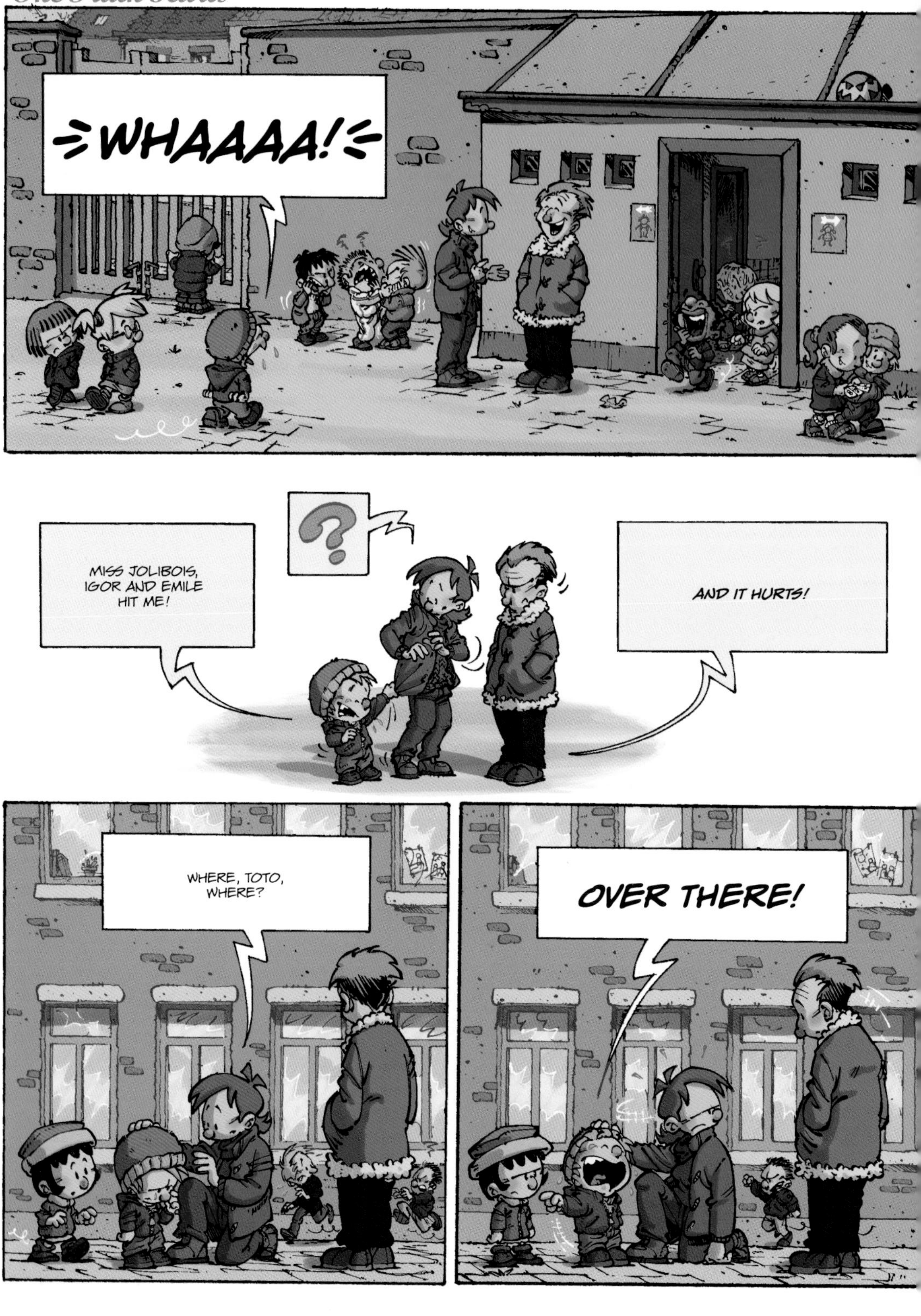
WHAAAA!
?
MISS JOLIBOIS, IGOR AND EMILE HIT ME!
AND IT HURTS!
WHERE, TOTO, WHERE?
OVER THERE!

"Truth or Dare"

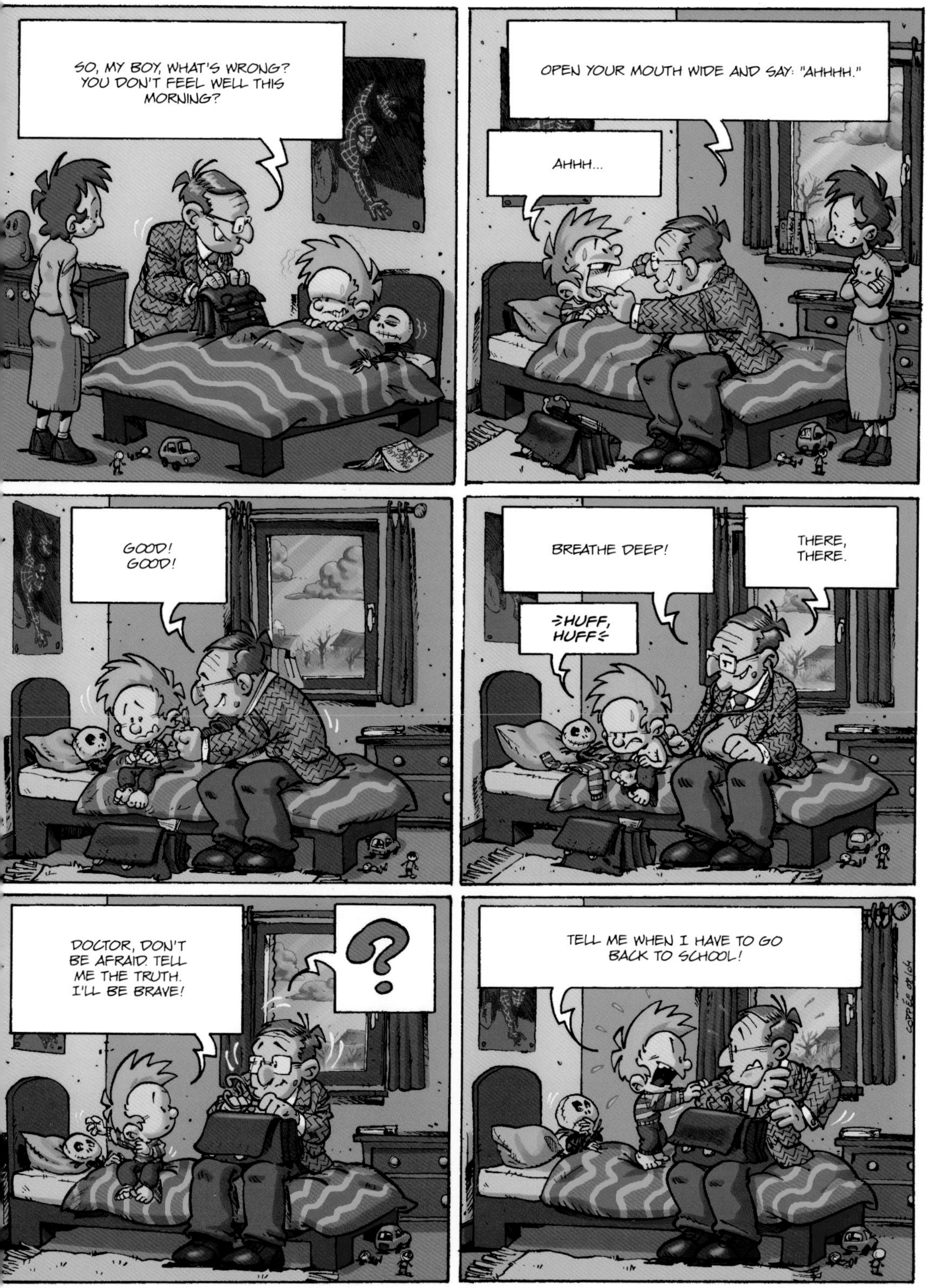
SO, MY BOY, WHAT'S WRONG? YOU DON'T FEEL WELL THIS MORNING?
OPEN YOUR MOUTH WIDE AND SAY: "AHHHH."
AHHH...
GOOD! GOOD!
BREATHE DEEP!
THERE, THERE.
=HUFF, HUFF=
DOCTOR, DON'T BE AFRAID. TELL ME THE TRUTH. I'LL BE BRAVE!
?
TELL ME WHEN I HAVE TO GO BACK TO SCHOOL!

"One Cousin Equals Two"

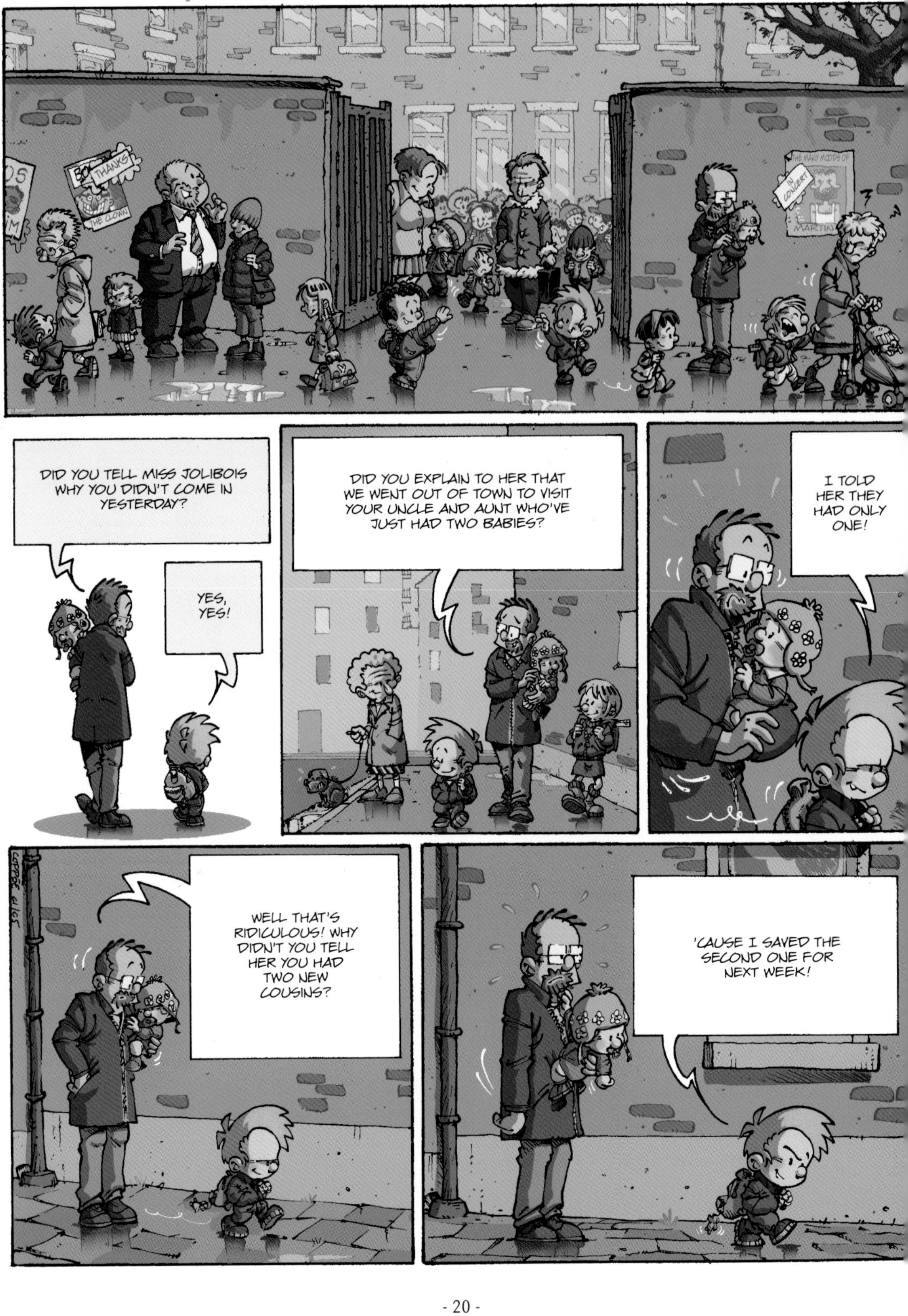
THANKS
THE CLOWN
THE MANY MOODS OF
IN CONCERT
DID YOU TELL MISS JOLIBOIS WHY YOU DIDN'T COME IN YESTERDAY?
YES, YES!
DID YOU EXPLAIN TO HER THAT WE WENT OUT OF TOWN TO VISIT YOUR UNCLE AND AUNT WHO'VE JUST HAD TWO BABIES?
I TOLD HER THEY HAD ONLY ONE!
WELL THAT'S RIDICULOUS! WHY DIDN'T YOU TELL HER YOU HAD TWO NEW COUSINS?
'CAUSE I SAVED THE SECOND ONE FOR NEXT WEEK!

"At The Risk of Knowing"

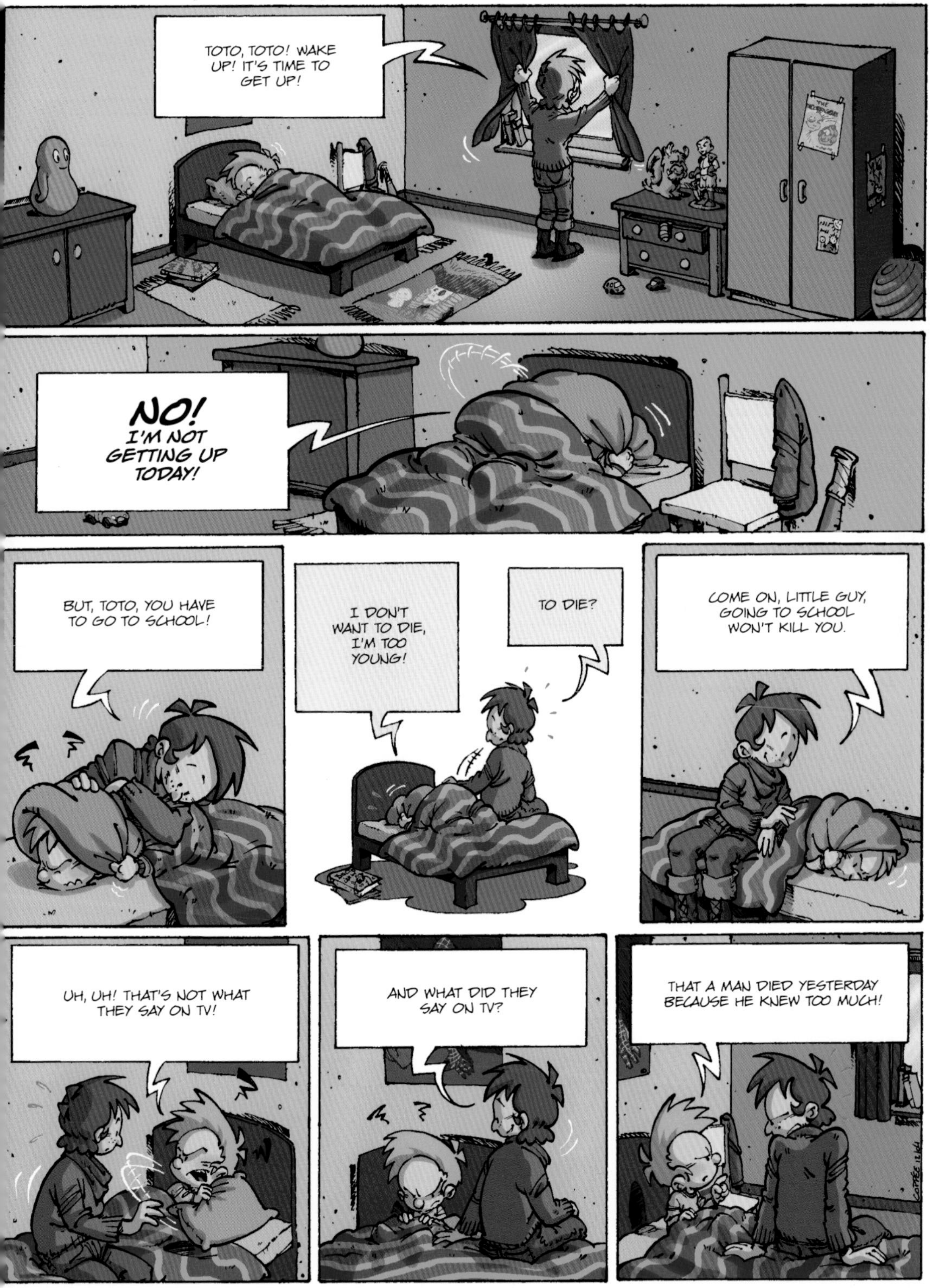
TOTO, TOTO! WAKE UP! IT'S TIME TO GET UP!
NO! I'M NOT GETTING UP TODAY!
BUT, TOTO, YOU HAVE TO GO TO SCHOOL!
I DON'T WANT TO DIE, I'M TOO YOUNG!
TO DIE?
COME ON, LITTLE GUY, GOING TO SCHOOL WON'T KILL YOU.
UH, UH! THAT'S NOT WHAT THEY SAY ON TV!
AND WHAT DID THEY SAY ON TV?
THAT A MAN DIED YESTERDAY BECAUSE HE KNEW TOO MUCH!

"Cyclotherapy"

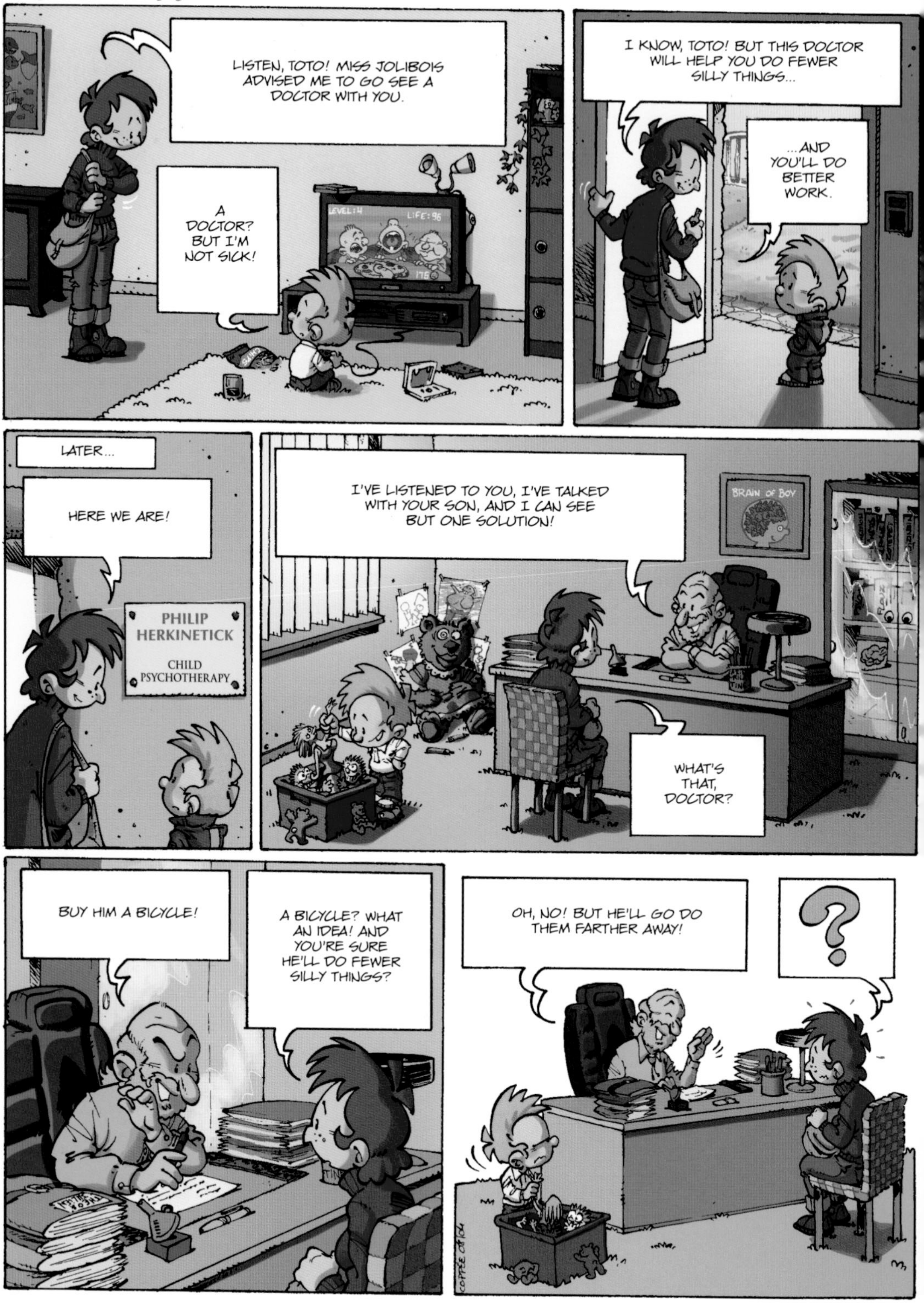
LISTEN, TOTO! MISS JOLIBOIS ADVISED ME TO GO SEE A DOCTOR WITH YOU.
A DOCTOR? BUT I'M NOT SICK!
LEVEL: 4
LIFE: 96
175
CHIPS
I KNOW, TOTO! BUT THIS DOCTOR WILL HELP YOU DO FEWER SILLY THINGS...
...AND YOU'LL DO BETTER WORK.
LATER...
HERE WE ARE!
PHILIP HERKINETICK
CHILD PSYCHOTHERAPY
I'VE LISTENED TO YOU, I'VE TALKED WITH YOUR SON, AND I CAN SEE BUT ONE SOLUTION!
BRAIN OF BOY
WHAT'S THAT, DOCTOR?
BUY HIM A BICYCLE!
A BICYCLE? WHAT AN IDEA! AND YOU'RE SURE HE'LL DO FEWER SILLY THINGS?
OH, NO! BUT HE'LL GO DO THEM FARTHER AWAY!
?

"Forgery"

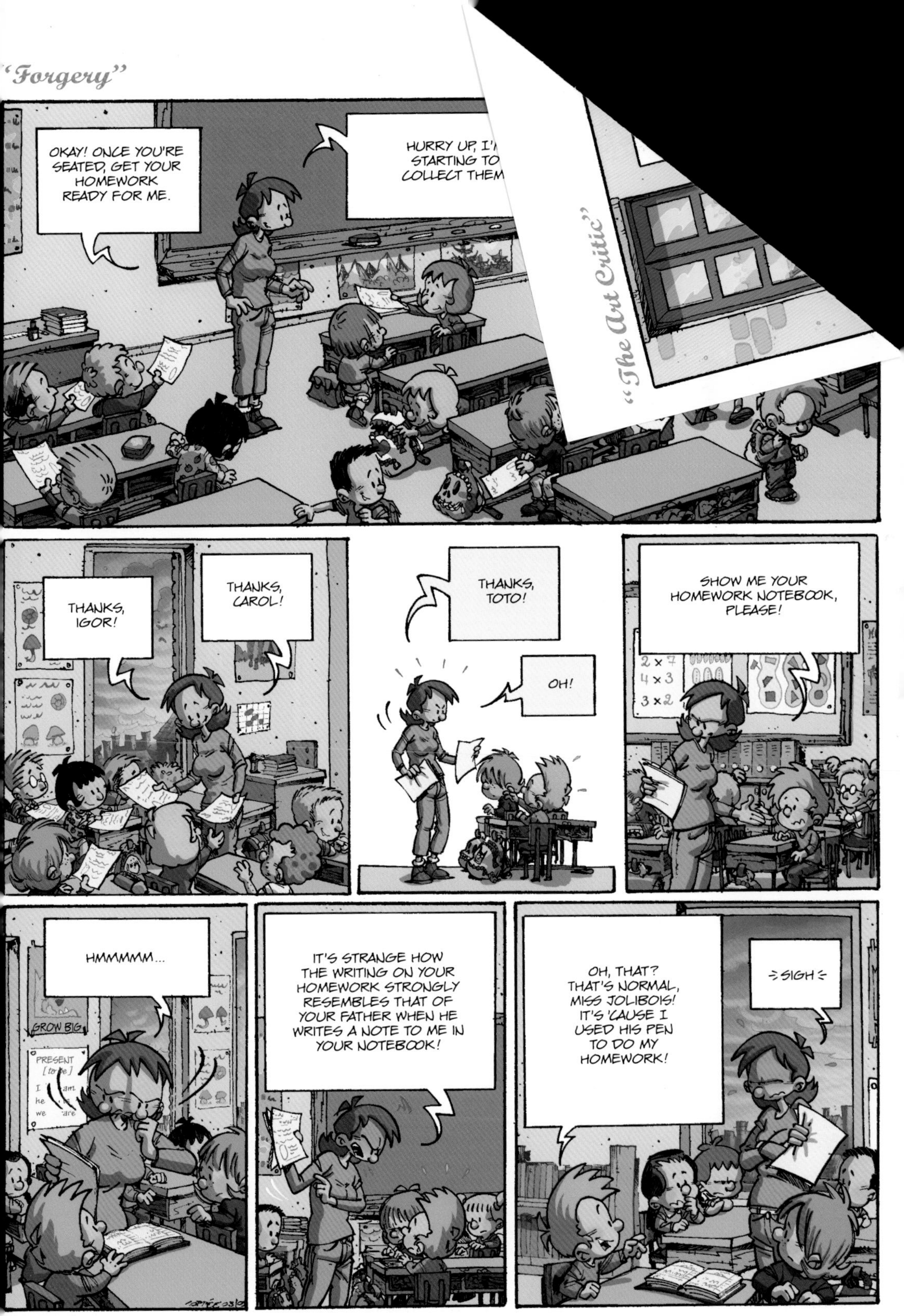

OKAY! ONCE YOU'RE SEATED, GET YOUR HOMEWORK READY FOR ME.
HURRY UP, I'M STARTING TO COLLECT THEM!
"The Art Critic"
THANKS, IGOR!
THANKS, CAROL!
THANKS, TOTO!
OH!
SHOW ME YOUR HOMEWORK NOTEBOOK, PLEASE!
2 x 7
4 x 3
3 x 2
HMMMMM...
GROW BIG
PRESENT
[to be]
I am
he
we are
IT'S STRANGE HOW THE WRITING ON YOUR HOMEWORK STRONGLY RESEMBLES THAT OF YOUR FATHER WHEN HE WRITES A NOTE TO ME IN YOUR NOTEBOOK!
OH, THAT? THAT'S NORMAL, MISS JOLIBOIS! IT'S 'CAUSE I USED HIS PEN TO DO MY HOMEWORK!
SIGH

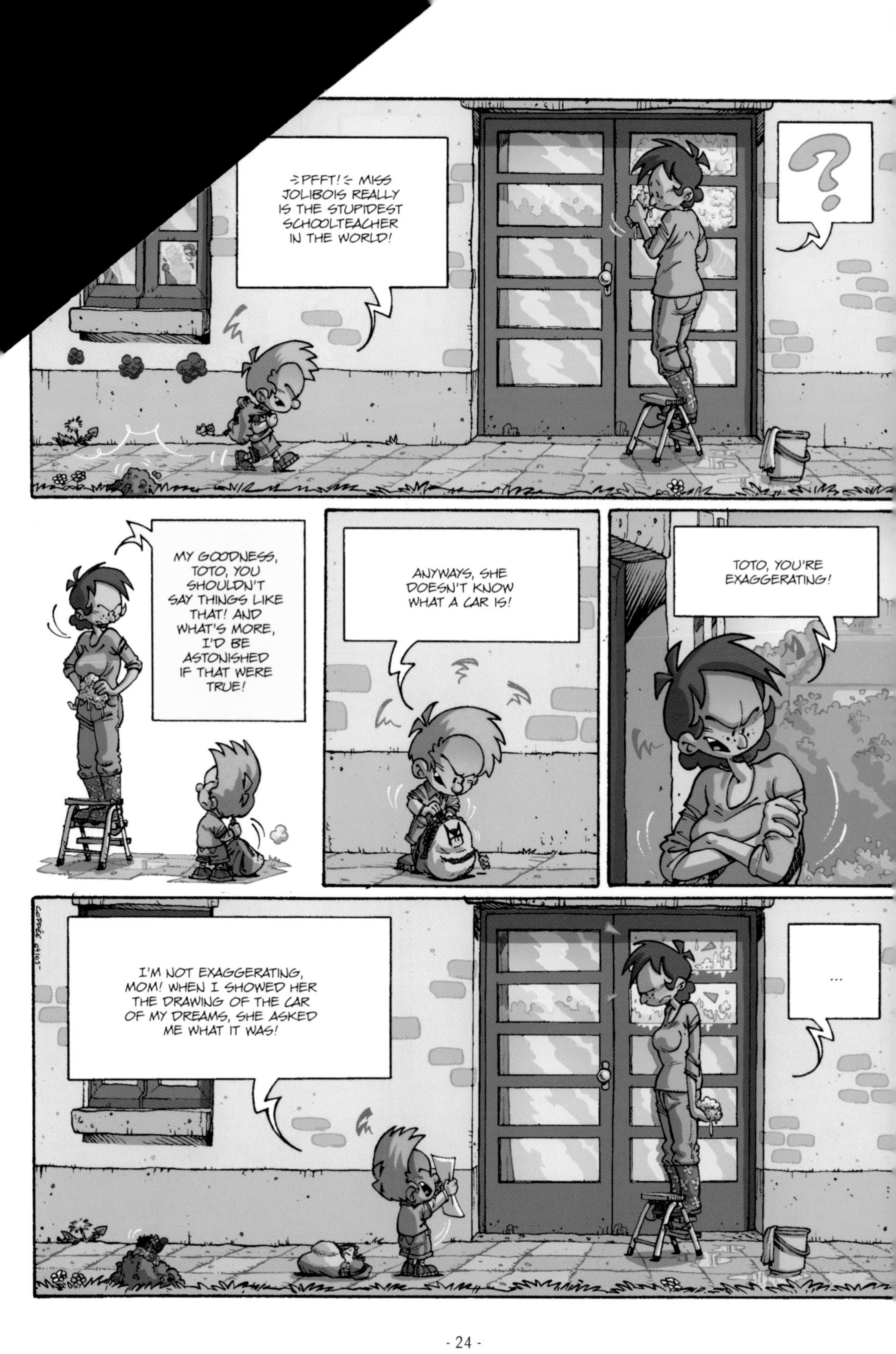
⇉PFFT!⇇ MISS JOLIBOIS REALLY IS THE STUPIDEST SCHOOLTEACHER IN THE WORLD!
?
MY GOODNESS, TOTO, YOU SHOULDN'T SAY THINGS LIKE THAT! AND WHAT'S MORE, I'D BE ASTONISHED IF THAT WERE TRUE!
ANYWAYS, SHE DOESN'T KNOW WHAT A CAR IS!
TOTO, YOU'RE EXAGGERATING!
I'M NOT EXAGGERATING, MOM! WHEN I SHOWED HER THE DRAWING OF THE CAR OF MY DREAMS, SHE ASKED ME WHAT IT WAS!
...

"Happiness: Future Tense"

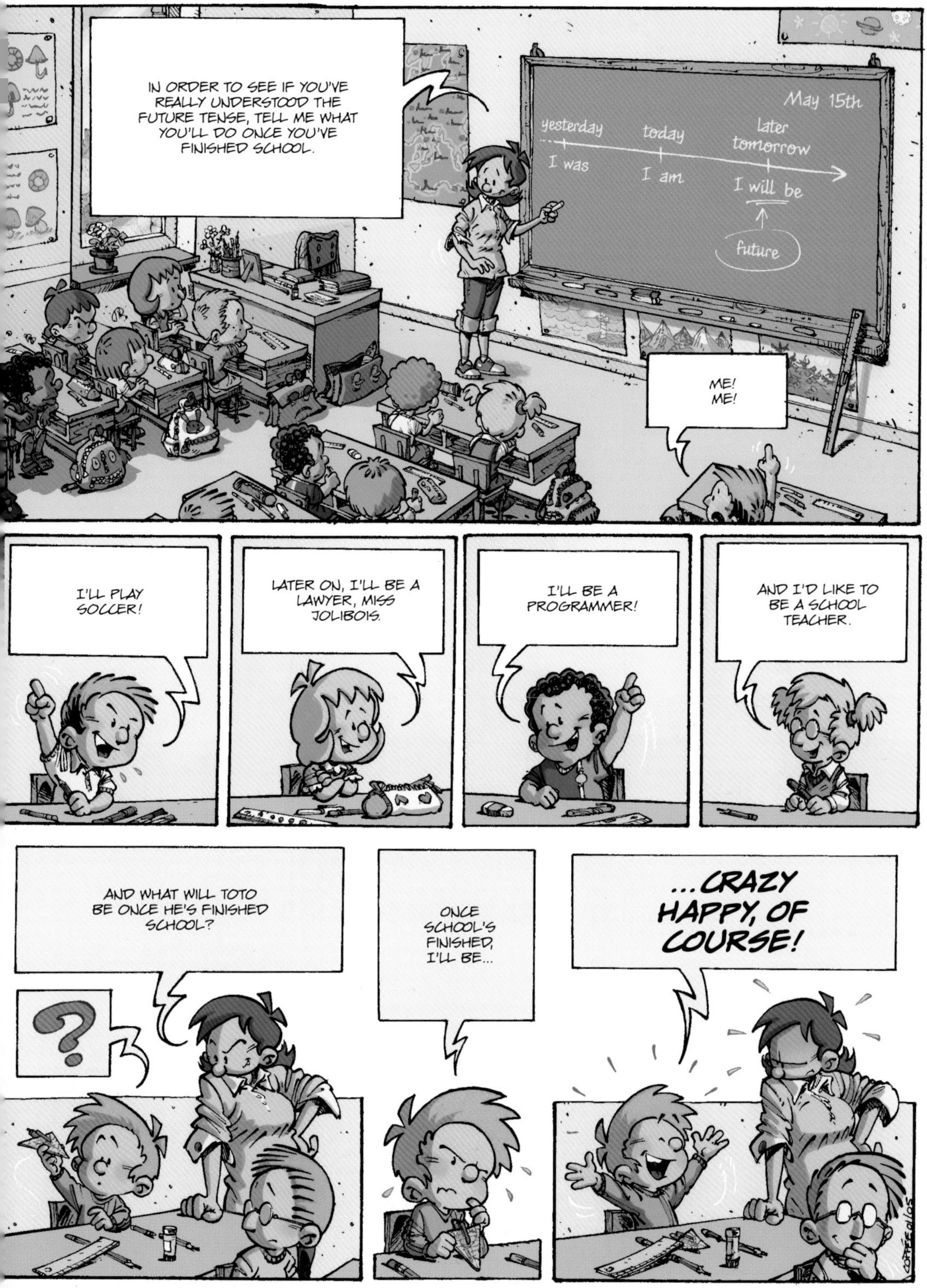
IN ORDER TO SEE IF YOU'VE REALLY UNDERSTOOD THE FUTURE TENSE, TELL ME WHAT YOU'LL DO ONCE YOU'VE FINISHED SCHOOL.
May 15th
yesterday
today
later tomorrow
I was
I am
I will be
future
ME! ME!
I'LL PLAY SOCCER!
LATER ON, I'LL BE A LAWYER, MISS JOLIBOIS.
I'LL BE A PROGRAMMER!
AND I'D LIKE TO BE A SCHOOL TEACHER.
AND WHAT WILL TOTO BE ONCE HE'S FINISHED SCHOOL?
?
ONCE SCHOOL'S FINISHED, I'LL BE...
...CRAZY HAPPY, OF COURSE!

"Expert Counting"

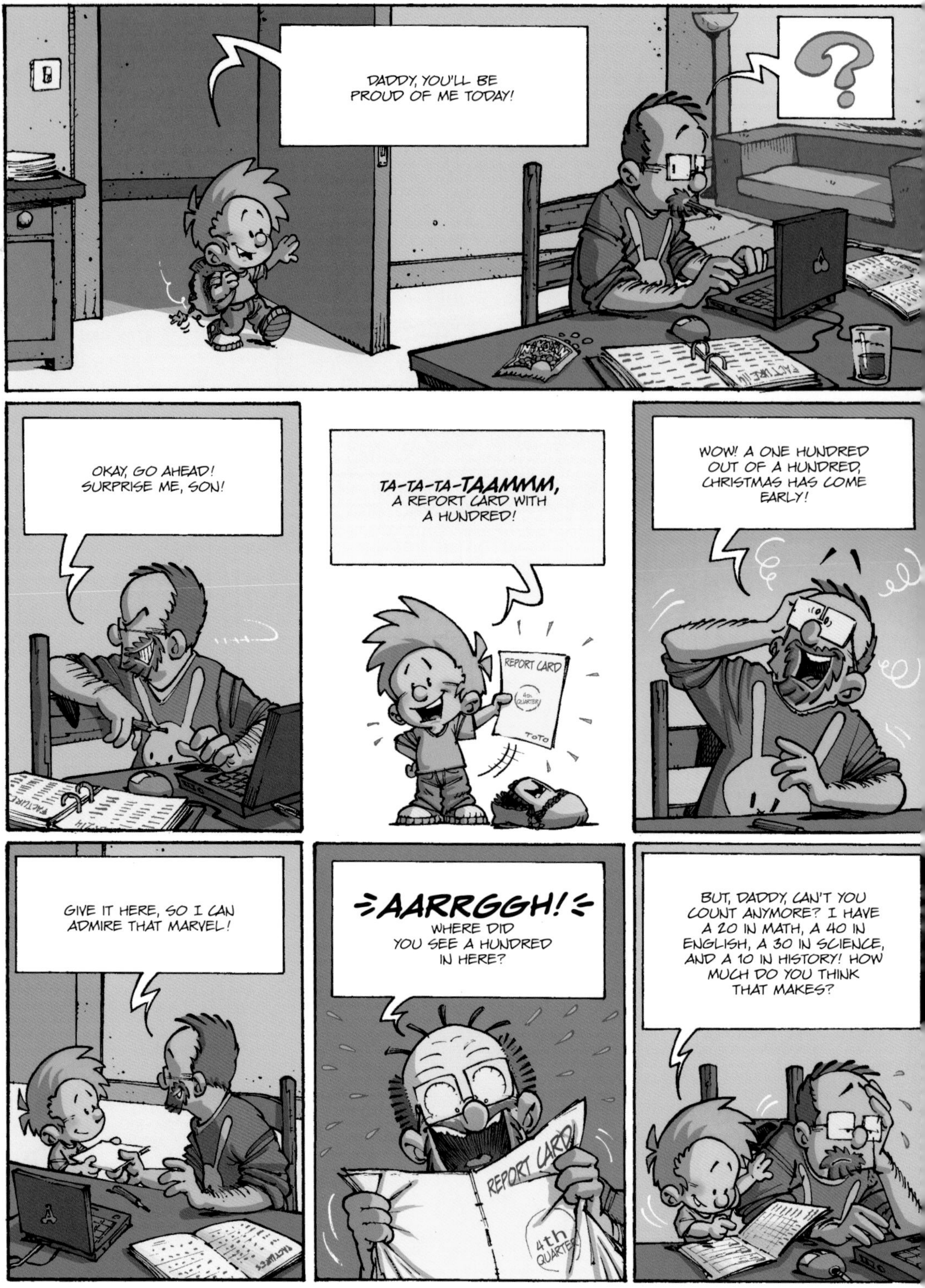
DADDY, YOU'LL BE PROUD OF ME TODAY!
?
OKAY, GO AHEAD! SURPRISE ME, SON!
TA-TA-TA-TAAMMM, A REPORT CARD WITH A HUNDRED!
REPORT CARD
TOTO
WOW! A ONE HUNDRED OUT OF A HUNDRED, CHRISTMAS HAS COME EARLY!
GIVE IT HERE, SO I CAN ADMIRE THAT MARVEL!
AARRGGH! WHERE DID YOU SEE A HUNDRED IN HERE?
REPORT CARD
4th QUARTER
BUT, DADDY, CAN'T YOU COUNT ANYMORE? I HAVE A 20 IN MATH, A 40 IN ENGLISH, A 30 IN SCIENCE, AND A 10 IN HISTORY! HOW MUCH DO YOU THINK THAT MAKES?

"A Knee-Slapper"

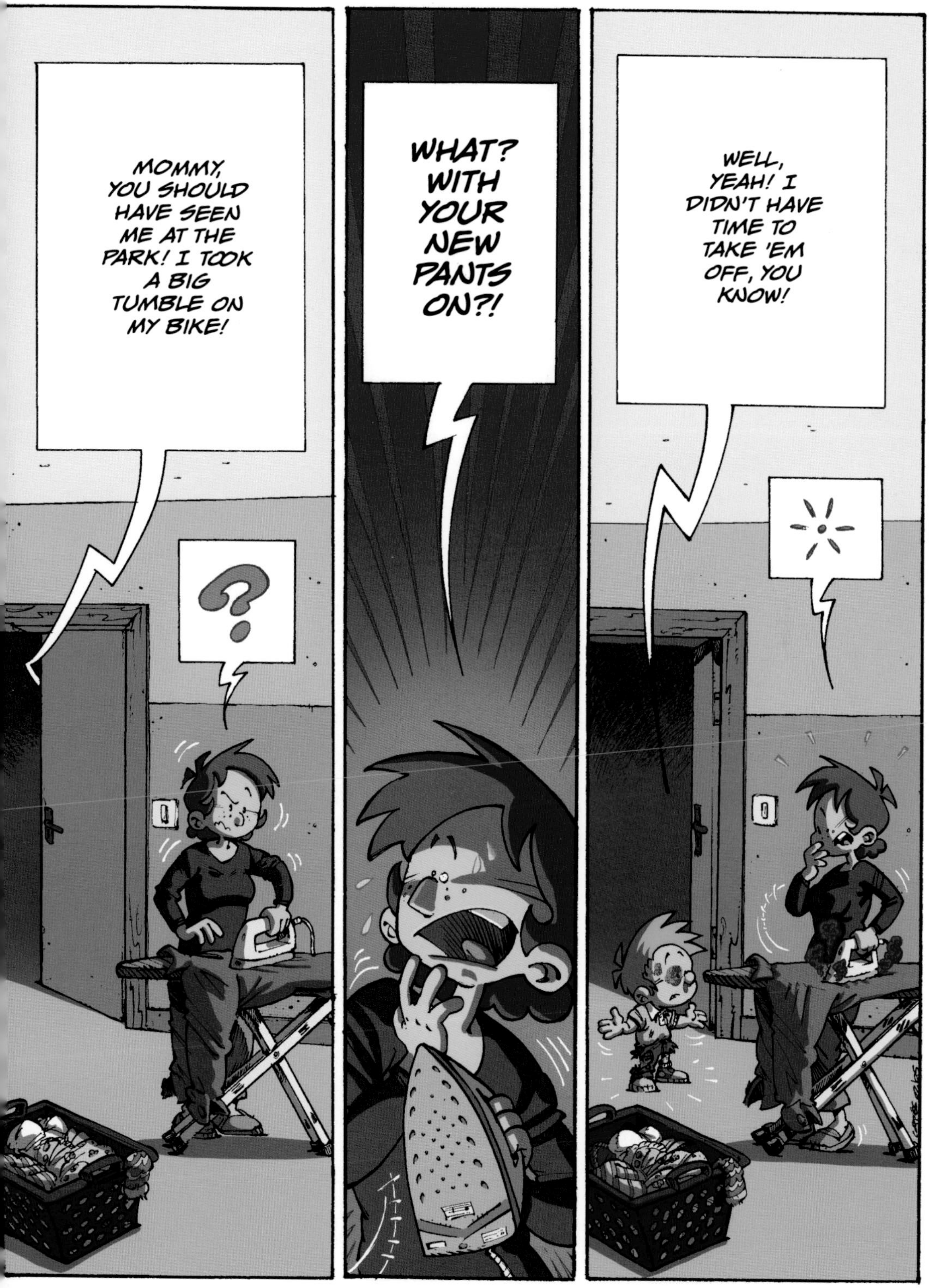
MOMMY, YOU SHOULD HAVE SEEN ME AT THE PARK! I TOOK A BIG TUMBLE ON MY BIKE!
?
WHAT? WITH YOUR NEW PANTS ON?!
WELL, YEAH! I DIDN'T HAVE TIME TO TAKE 'EM OFF, YOU KNOW!

"Joking Alone"

HEY!
PSSST
PSSSST
?
YOU'RE NOT IN BED?
YOU WERE GOING TO FORGET TO TAKE THIS!
WHAT'S THAT? YOUR BANK REPORT?
NO, NO, IT'S MY REPORT CARD, AND I'D LIKE MY MOM NOT TO FIND IT!

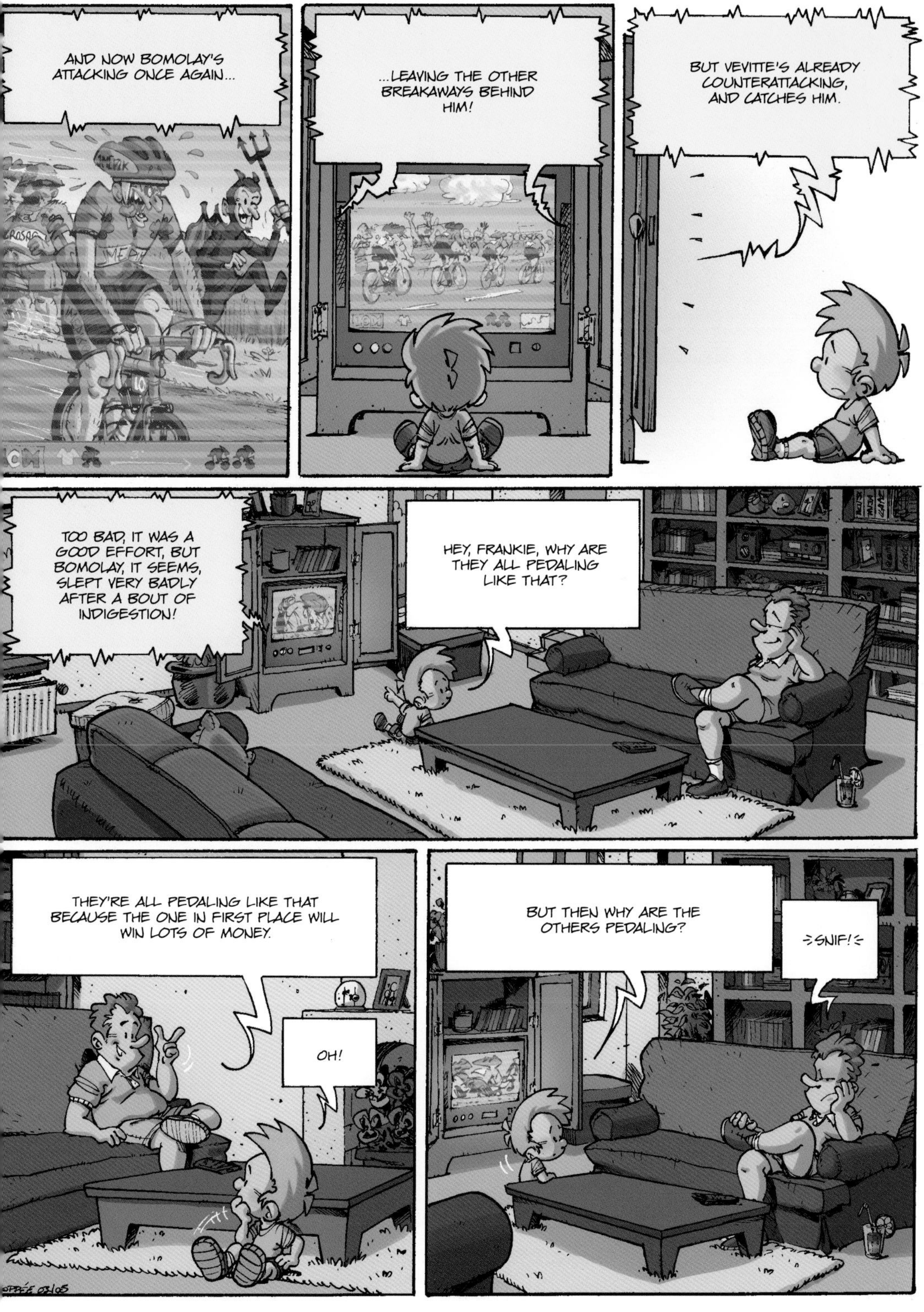
AND NOW BOMOLAY'S ATTACKING ONCE AGAIN...
...LEAVING THE OTHER BREAKAWAYS BEHIND HIM!
BUT VEVITTE'S ALREADY COUNTERATTACKING, AND CATCHES HIM.
TOO BAD, IT WAS A GOOD EFFORT, BUT BOMOLAY, IT SEEMS, SLEPT VERY BADLY AFTER A BOUT OF INDIGESTION!
HEY, FRANKIE, WHY ARE THEY ALL PEDALING LIKE THAT?
THEY'RE ALL PEDALING LIKE THAT BECAUSE THE ONE IN FIRST PLACE WILL WIN LOTS OF MONEY.
OH!
BUT THEN WHY ARE THE OTHERS PEDALING?
SNIF!

"Quiet on the Set!"

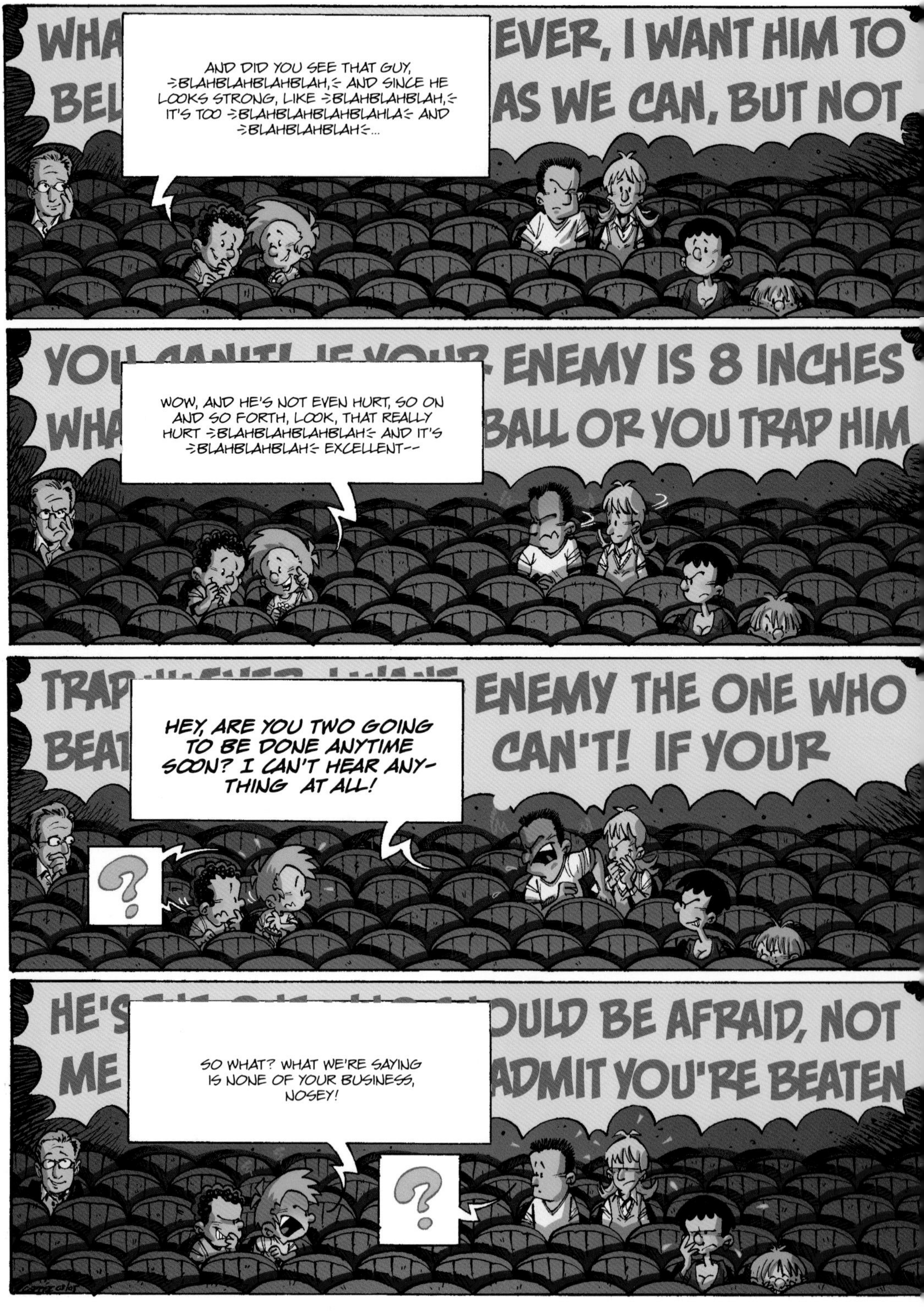

WHA EVER, I WANT HIM TO
BE AS WE CAN, BUT NOT
AND DID YOU SEE THAT GUY, ⇒BLAHBLAHBLAHBLAH,⇐ AND SINCE HE LOOKS STRONG, LIKE ⇒BLAHBLAHBLAH,⇐ IT'S TOO ⇒BLAHBLAHBLAHBLAHLA⇐ AND ⇒BLAHBLAHBLAH⇐...
YOU ENEMY IS 8 INCHES
WHA BALL OR YOU TRAP HIM
WOW, AND HE'S NOT EVEN HURT, SO ON AND SO FORTH, LOOK, THAT REALLY HURT ⇒BLAHBLAHBLAHBLAH⇐ AND IT'S ⇒BLAHBLAHBLAH⇐ EXCELLENT--
TRAP ENEMY THE ONE WHO
BEAT CAN'T! IF YOUR
HEY, ARE YOU TWO GOING TO BE DONE ANYTIME SOON? I CAN'T HEAR ANY-THING AT ALL!
?
HE'S OULD BE AFRAID, NOT
ME ADMIT YOU'RE BEATEN
SO WHAT? WHAT WE'RE SAYING IS NONE OF YOUR BUSINESS, NOSEY!
?

"I Scream, You Scream, We All..."

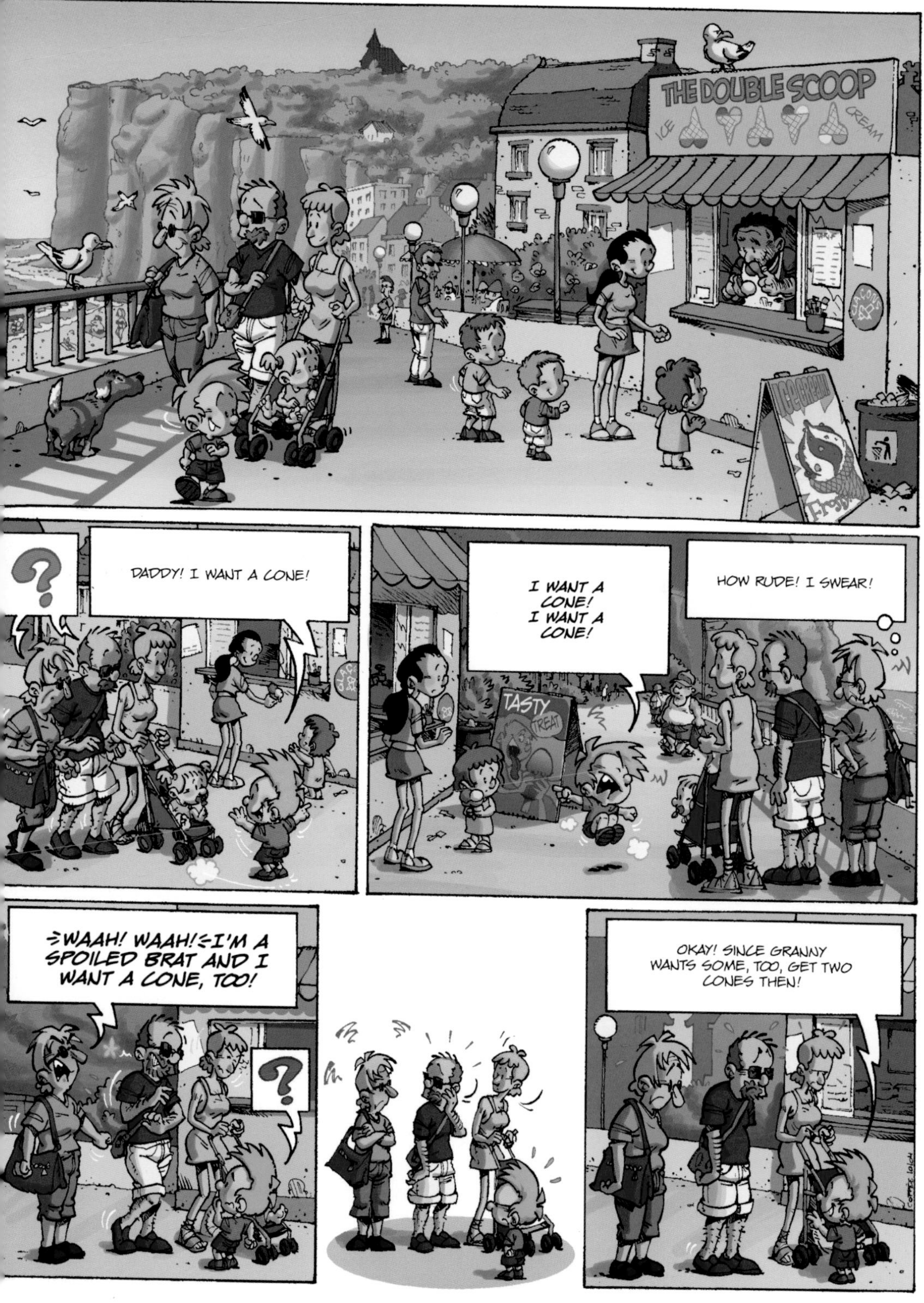
THE DOUBLE SCOOP
ICE
CREAM
ICE CREAM
TASTY
TREAT
?
DADDY! I WANT A CONE!
I WANT A CONE!
I WANT A CONE!
HOW RUDE! I SWEAR!
=WAAH! WAAH!= I'M A SPOILED BRAT AND I WANT A CONE, TOO!
?
OKAY! SINCE GRANNY WANTS SOME, TOO, GET TWO CONES THEN!

"A Dunce on the Go"

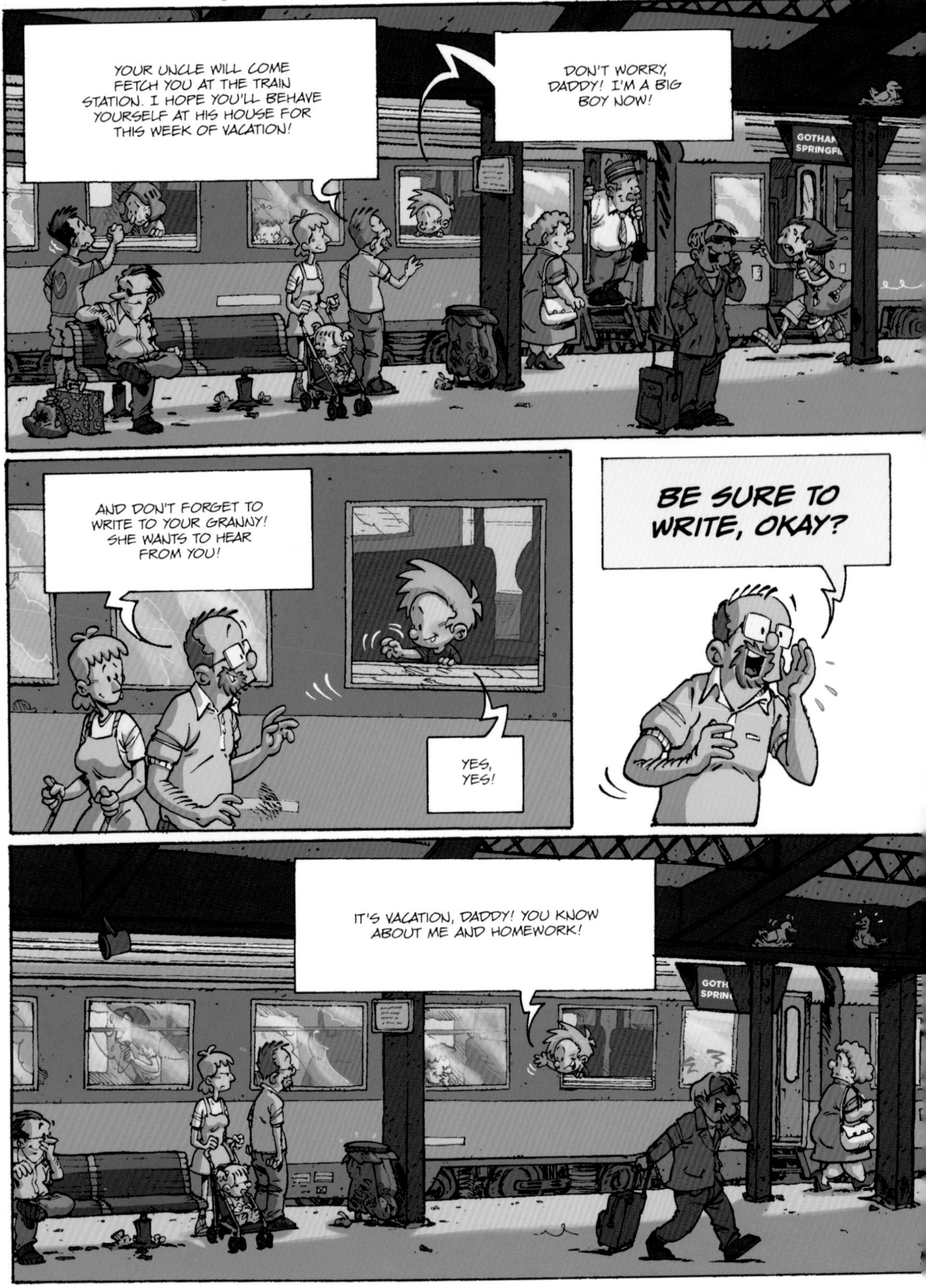
YOUR UNCLE WILL COME FETCH YOU AT THE TRAIN STATION. I HOPE YOU'LL BEHAVE YOURSELF AT HIS HOUSE FOR THIS WEEK OF VACATION!
DON'T WORRY, DADDY! I'M A BIG BOY NOW!
GOTHAM SPRINGFI
AND DON'T FORGET TO WRITE TO YOUR GRANNY! SHE WANTS TO HEAR FROM YOU!
YES, YES!
BE SURE TO WRITE, OKAY?
IT'S VACATION, DADDY! YOU KNOW ABOUT ME AND HOMEWORK!

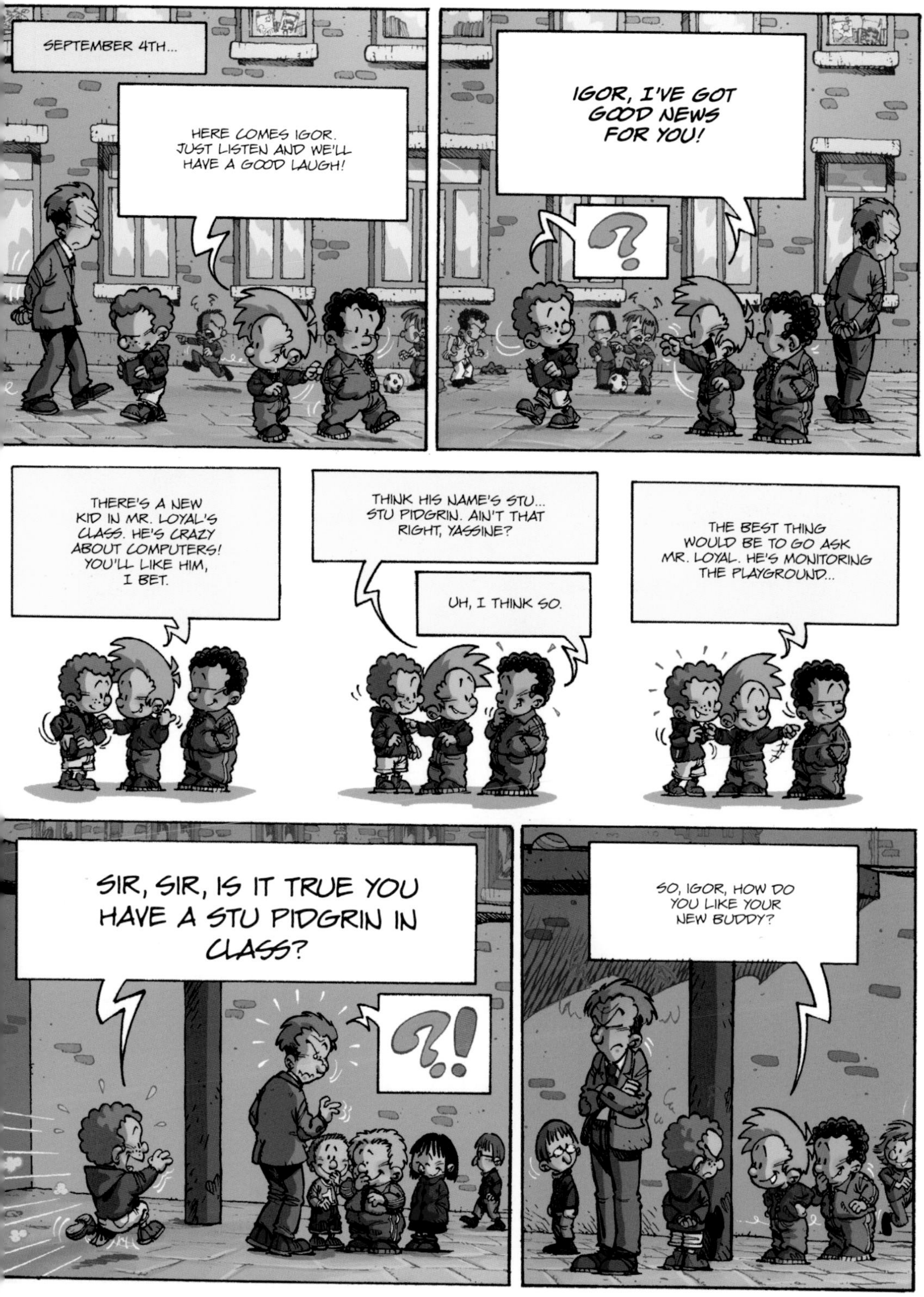
SEPTEMBER 4TH...
HERE COMES IGOR. JUST LISTEN AND WE'LL HAVE A GOOD LAUGH!
IGOR, I'VE GOT GOOD NEWS FOR YOU!
?
THERE'S A NEW KID IN MR. LOYAL'S CLASS. HE'S CRAZY ABOUT COMPUTERS! YOU'LL LIKE HIM, I BET.
THINK HIS NAME'S STU... STU PIDGRIN. AIN'T THAT RIGHT, YASSINE?
UH, I THINK SO.
THE BEST THING WOULD BE TO GO ASK MR. LOYAL. HE'S MONITORING THE PLAYGROUND...
SIR, SIR, IS IT TRUE YOU HAVE A STU PIDGRIN IN CLASS?
?!
SO, IGOR, HOW DO YOU LIKE YOUR NEW BUDDY?

"The Soldier's Return"

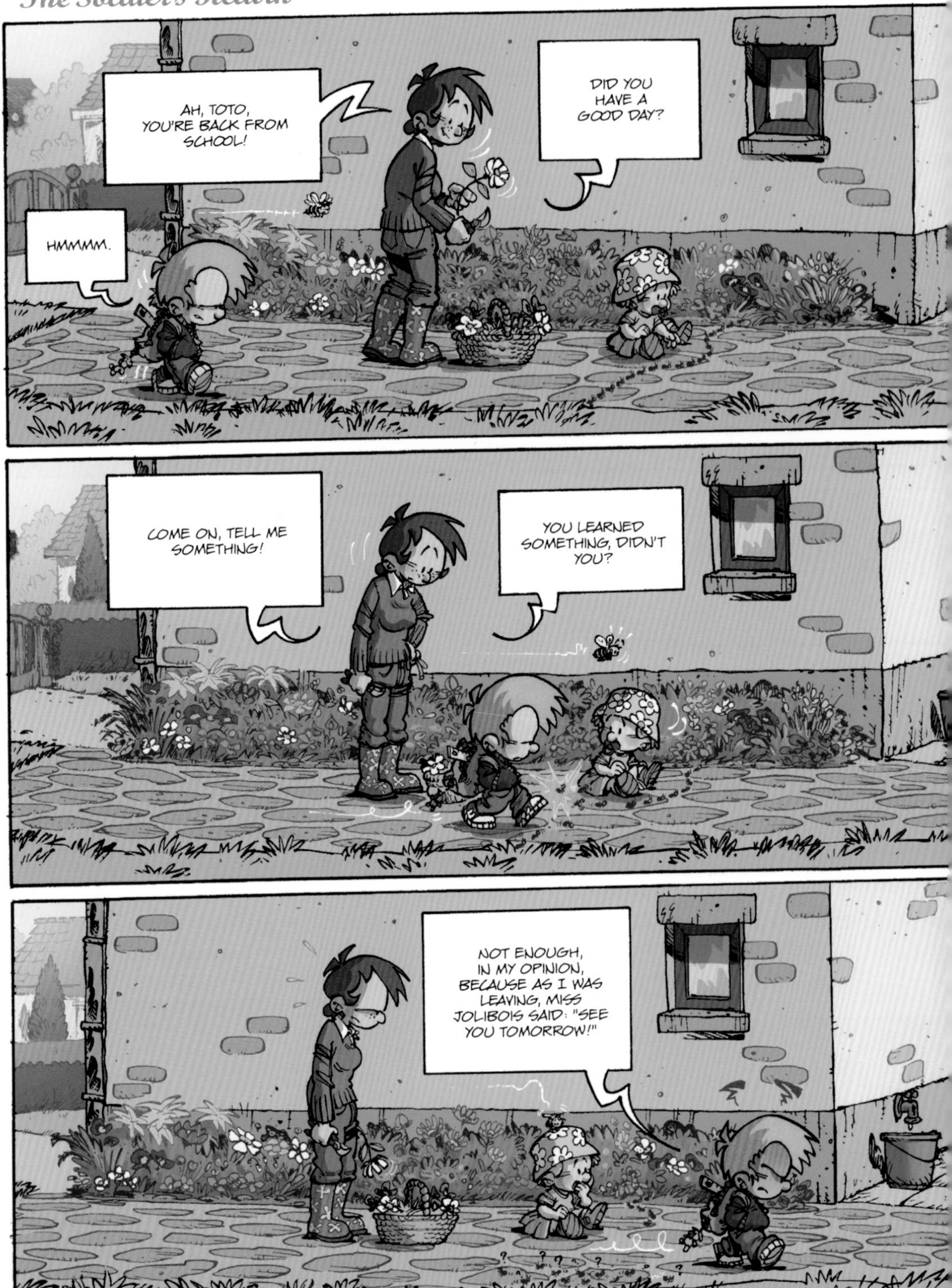
AH, TOTO, YOU'RE BACK FROM SCHOOL!
DID YOU HAVE A GOOD DAY?
HMMMM.
COME ON, TELL ME SOMETHING!
YOU LEARNED SOMETHING, DIDN'T YOU?
NOT ENOUGH, IN MY OPINION, BECAUSE AS I WAS LEAVING, MISS JOLIBOIS SAID: "SEE YOU TOMORROW!"

"Laterality Failure"

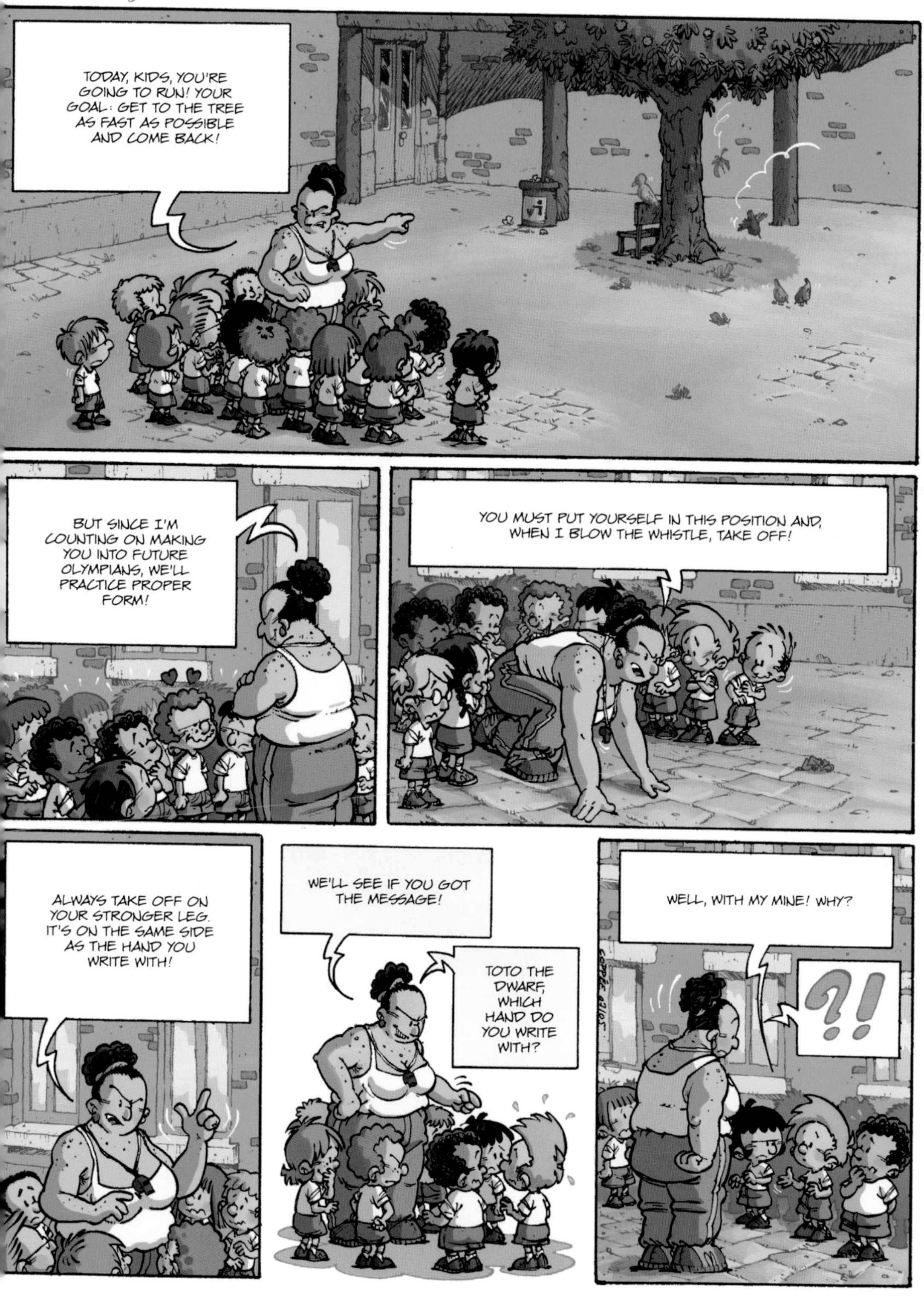
TODAY, KIDS, YOU'RE GOING TO RUN! YOUR GOAL: GET TO THE TREE AS FAST AS POSSIBLE AND COME BACK!
BUT SINCE I'M COUNTING ON MAKING YOU INTO FUTURE OLYMPIANS, WE'LL PRACTICE PROPER FORM!
YOU MUST PUT YOURSELF IN THIS POSITION AND, WHEN I BLOW THE WHISTLE, TAKE OFF!
ALWAYS TAKE OFF ON YOUR STRONGER LEG. IT'S ON THE SAME SIDE AS THE HAND YOU WRITE WITH!
WE'LL SEE IF YOU GOT THE MESSAGE!
TOTO THE DWARF, WHICH HAND DO YOU WRITE WITH?
WELL, WITH MY MINE! WHY?
?!

"Dirty Hands"

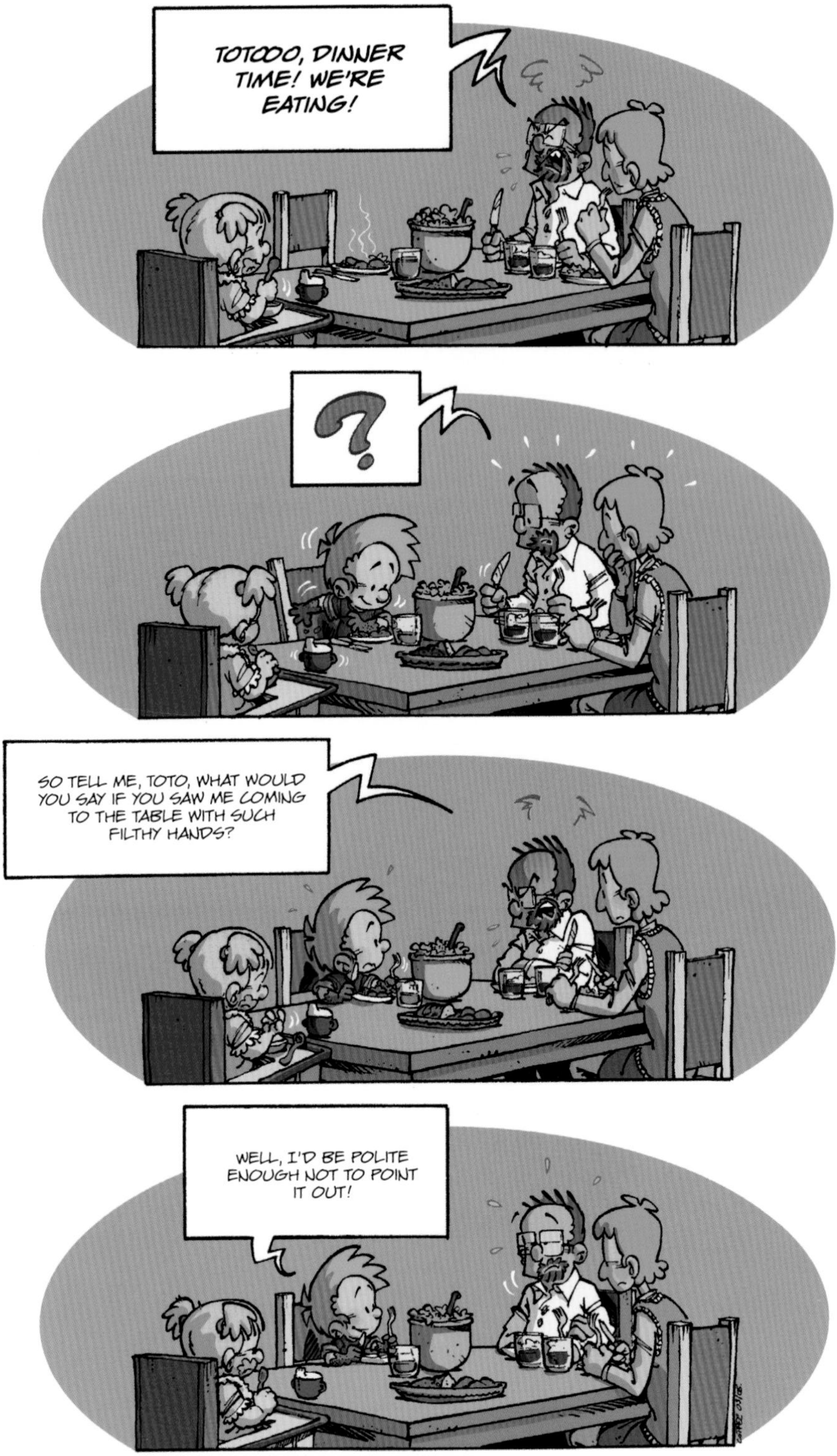
TOTOOO, DINNER TIME! WE'RE EATING!
?
SO TELL ME, TOTO, WHAT WOULD YOU SAY IF YOU SAW ME COMING TO THE TABLE WITH SUCH FILTHY HANDS?
WELL, I'D BE POLITE ENOUGH NOT TO POINT IT OUT!

"The Family Game"

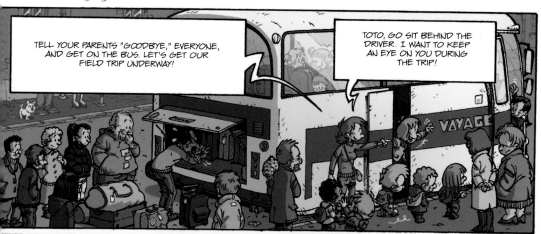

TELL YOUR PARENTS "GOODBYE," EVERYONE, AND GET ON THE BUS. LET'S GET OUR FIELD TRIP UNDERWAY!

TOTO, GO SIT BEHIND THE DRIVER. I WANT TO KEEP AN EYE ON YOU DURING THE TRIP!

WE CAN LEAVE, EVERYONE'S HERE!

LET'S GO THEN!

FARTHER ALONG...

...IF MY FATHER WAS A BULL AND MY MOTHER WAS A COW, I'D BE A CALF. IF MY FATHER WAS A BOAR AND MY MOTHER WAS A SOW, I'D BE A PIGLET...

MUCH FARTHER ALONG AND LATER...

...IF MY FATHER WAS A GANDER AND MY MOTHER WAS A GOOSE, I'D BE A GOSLING. IF MY FATHER WAS A ROOSTER AND MY MOTHER WAS A HEN, I'D BE A CHICK...

EVEN FARTHER ALONG...

...IF MY FATHER WAS A RAM AND MY MOTHER WAS A EWE, I'D BE A LAMB. IF MY FATHER WAS A WOLF AND MY MOTHER WAS A SHE-WOLF, I'D BE A CUB--

AND IF YOUR FATHER WAS A STUPID %$# AND YOUR MOTHER WAS A STUPID %!$@#, WHAT WOULD YOU BE THEN?!

A BUS DRIVER?

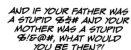
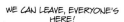

"A Very Teary First Night"

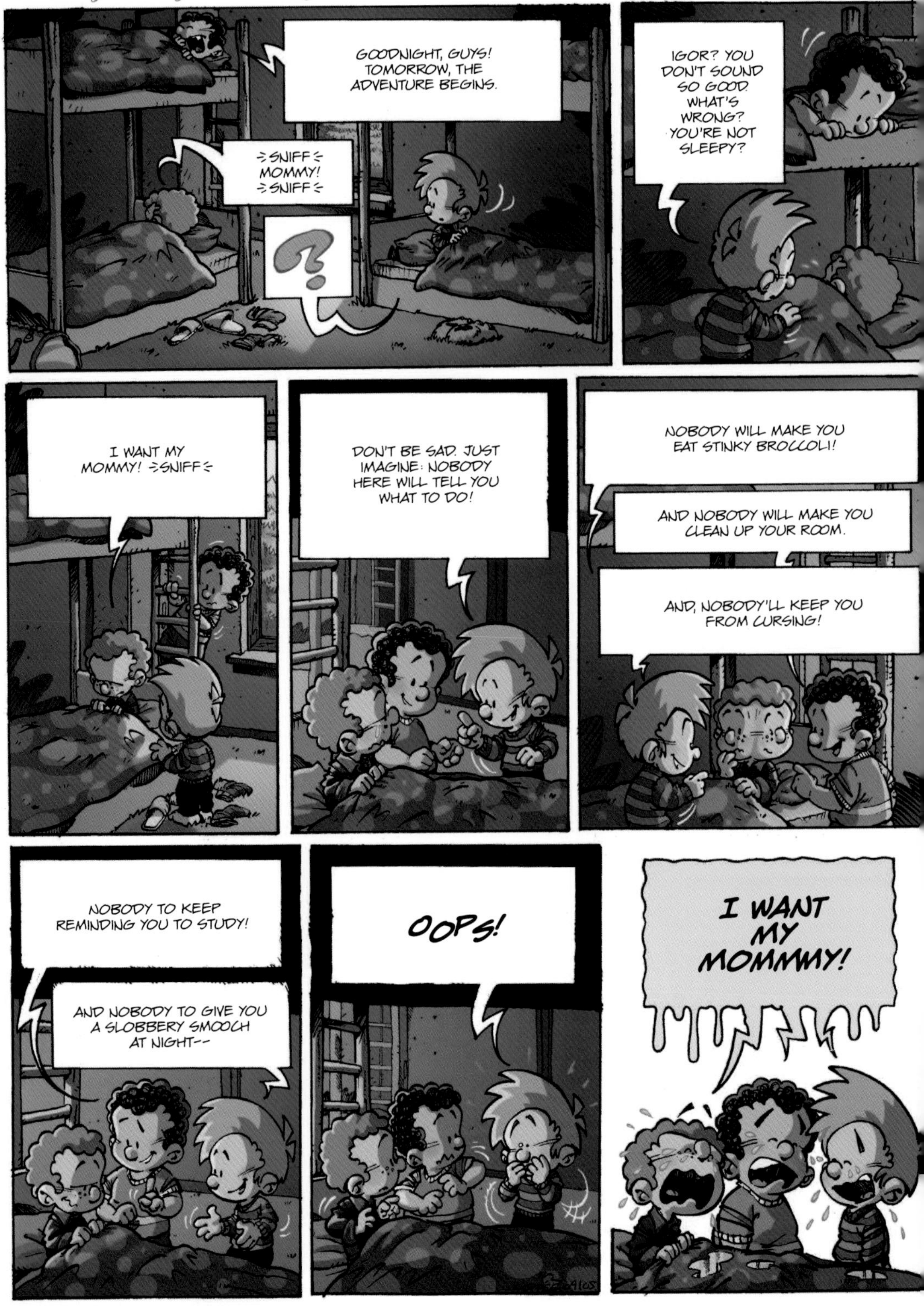
GOODNIGHT, GUYS! TOMORROW, THE ADVENTURE BEGINS.
=SNIFF= MOMMY! =SNIFF=
?
IGOR? YOU DON'T SOUND SO GOOD. WHAT'S WRONG? YOU'RE NOT SLEEPY?
I WANT MY MOMMY! =SNIFF=
DON'T BE SAD. JUST IMAGINE: NOBODY HERE WILL TELL YOU WHAT TO DO!
NOBODY WILL MAKE YOU EAT STINKY BROCCOLI!
AND NOBODY WILL MAKE YOU CLEAN UP YOUR ROOM.
AND, NOBODY'LL KEEP YOU FROM CURSING!
NOBODY TO KEEP REMINDING YOU TO STUDY!
AND NOBODY TO GIVE YOU A SLOBBERY SMOOCH AT NIGHT--
OOPS!
I WANT MY MOMMMY!

"Nature's Gifts"

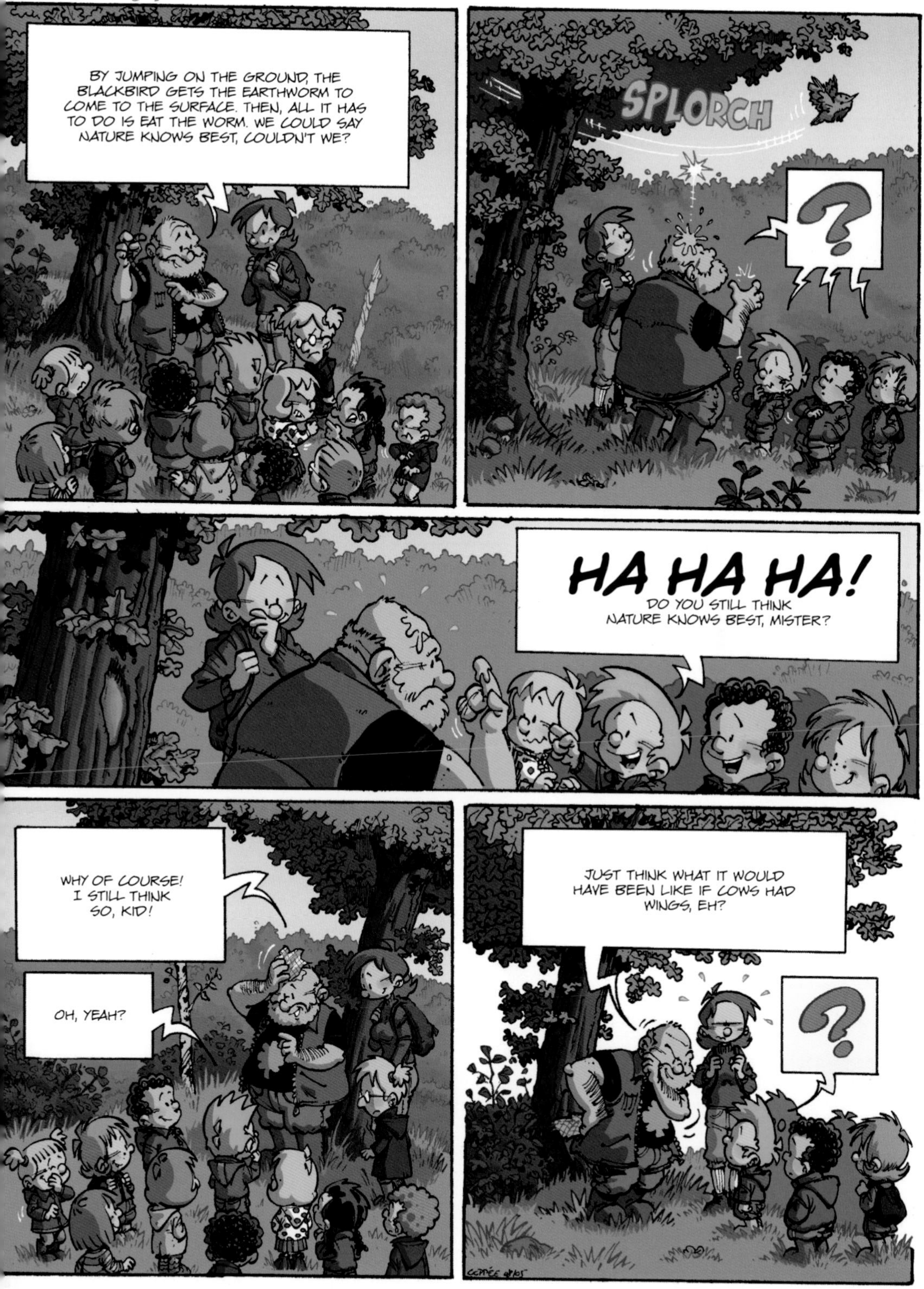
BY JUMPING ON THE GROUND, THE BLACKBIRD GETS THE EARTHWORM TO COME TO THE SURFACE. THEN, ALL IT HAS TO DO IS EAT THE WORM. WE COULD SAY NATURE KNOWS BEST, COULDN'T WE?
SPLORCH
?
HA HA HA! DO YOU STILL THINK NATURE KNOWS BEST, MISTER?
WHY OF COURSE! I STILL THINK SO, KID!
OH, YEAH?
JUST THINK WHAT IT WOULD HAVE BEEN LIKE IF COWS HAD WINGS, EH?
?

"Tracks and Traces"

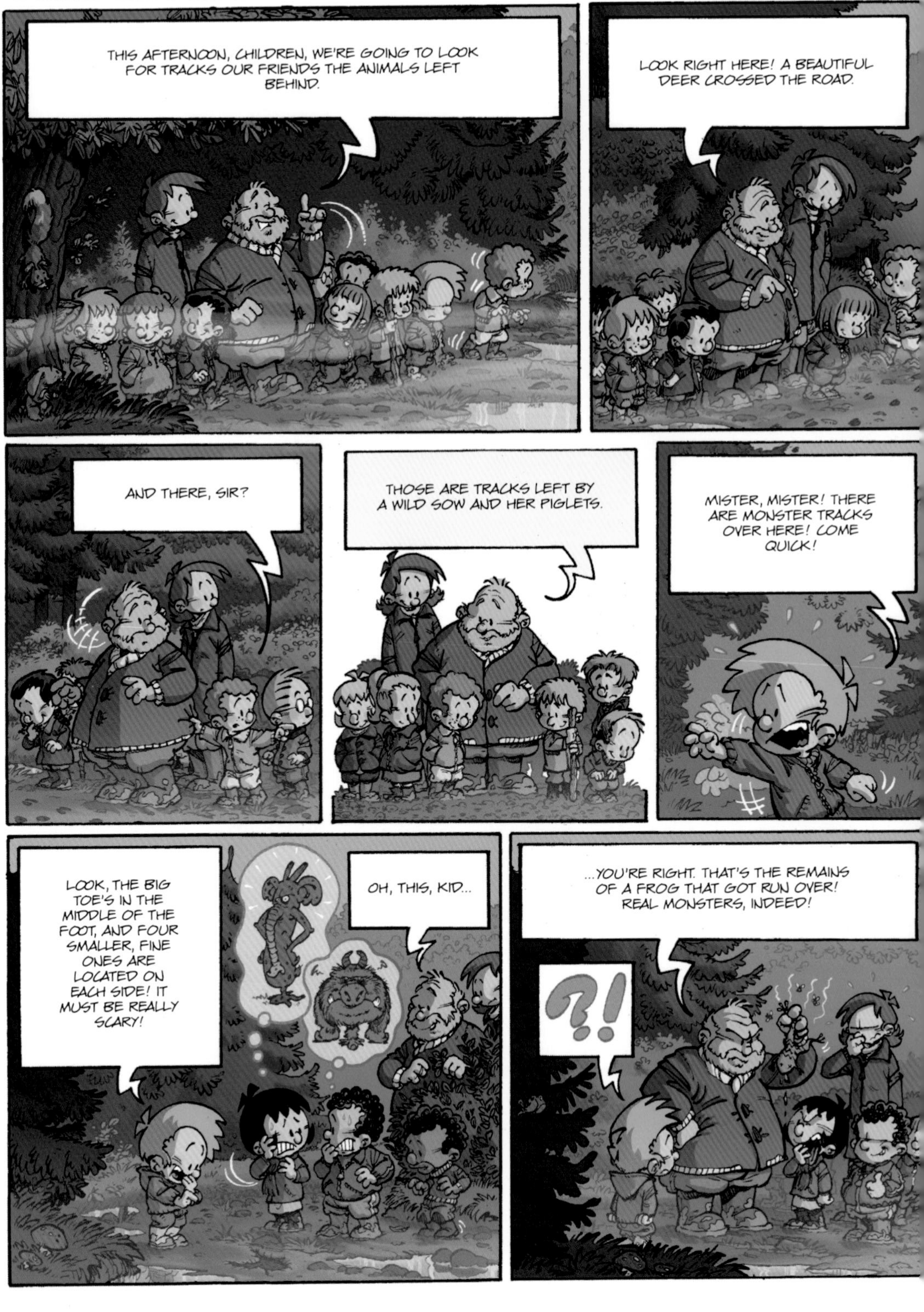
THIS AFTERNOON, CHILDREN, WE'RE GOING TO LOOK FOR TRACKS OUR FRIENDS THE ANIMALS LEFT BEHIND.
LOOK RIGHT HERE! A BEAUTIFUL DEER CROSSED THE ROAD.
AND THERE, SIR?
THOSE ARE TRACKS LEFT BY A WILD SOW AND HER PIGLETS.
MISTER, MISTER! THERE ARE MONSTER TRACKS OVER HERE! COME QUICK!
LOOK, THE BIG TOE'S IN THE MIDDLE OF THE FOOT, AND FOUR SMALLER, FINE ONES ARE LOCATED ON EACH SIDE! IT MUST BE REALLY SCARY!
OH, THIS, KID...
...YOU'RE RIGHT. THAT'S THE REMAINS OF A FROG THAT GOT RUN OVER! REAL MONSTERS, INDEED!
?!

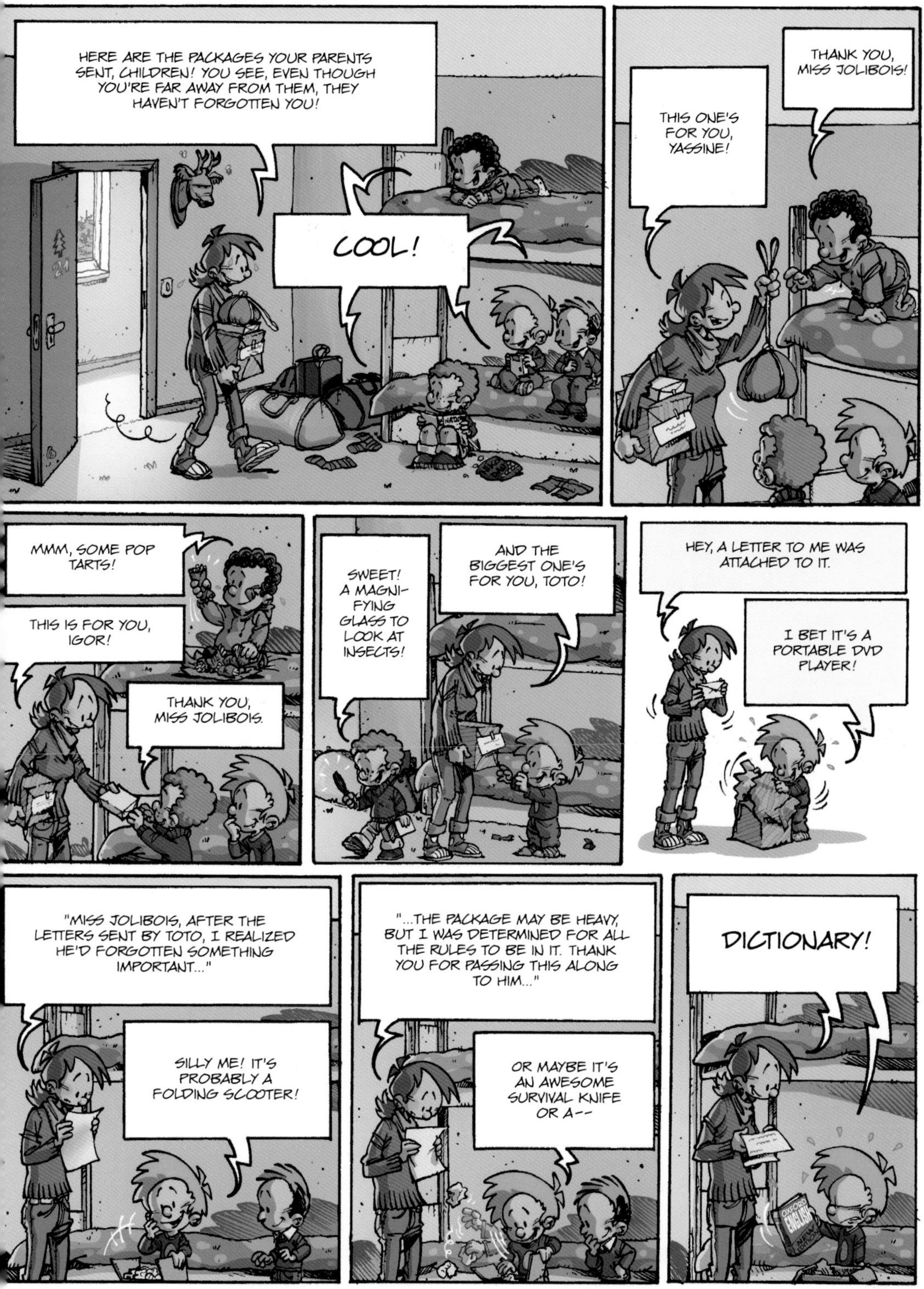
HERE ARE THE PACKAGES YOUR PARENTS SENT, CHILDREN! YOU SEE, EVEN THOUGH YOU'RE FAR AWAY FROM THEM, THEY HAVEN'T FORGOTTEN YOU!
COOL!
THIS ONE'S FOR YOU, YASSINE!
THANK YOU, MISS JOLIBOIS!
MMM, SOME POP TARTS!
THIS IS FOR YOU, IGOR!
THANK YOU, MISS JOLIBOIS.
SWEET! A MAGNI-FYING GLASS TO LOOK AT INSECTS!
AND THE BIGGEST ONE'S FOR YOU, TOTO!
HEY, A LETTER TO ME WAS ATTACHED TO IT.
I BET IT'S A PORTABLE DVD PLAYER!
"MISS JOLIBOIS, AFTER THE LETTERS SENT BY TOTO, I REALIZED HE'D FORGOTTEN SOMETHING IMPORTANT..."
SILLY ME! IT'S PROBABLY A FOLDING SCOOTER!
"...THE PACKAGE MAY BE HEAVY, BUT I WAS DETERMINED FOR ALL THE RULES TO BE IN IT. THANK YOU FOR PASSING THIS ALONG TO HIM..."
OR MAYBE IT'S AN AWESOME SURVIVAL KNIFE OR A--
DICTIONARY!
OXFORD ENGLISH

"Hunting with Dunces"

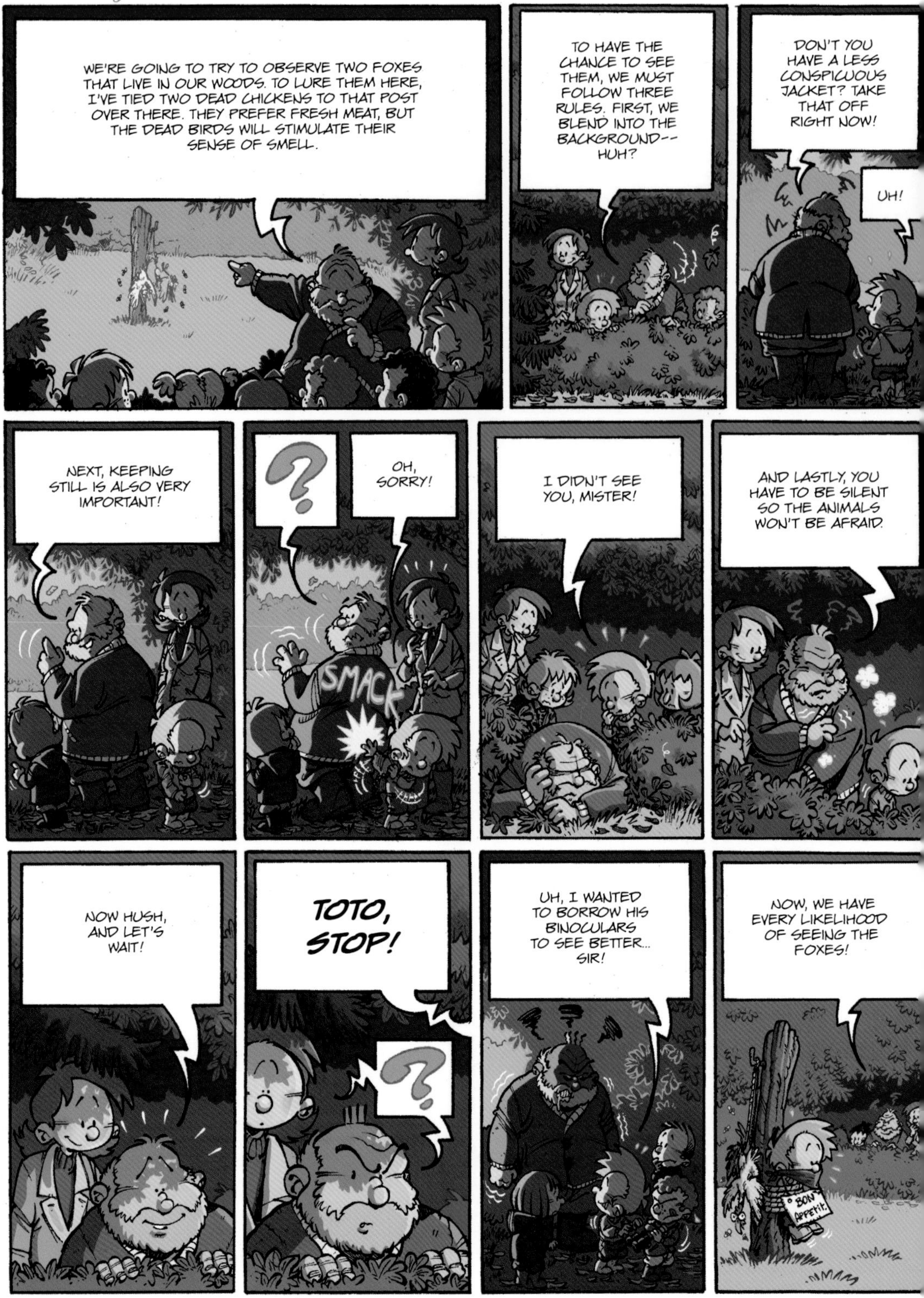
WE'RE GOING TO TRY TO OBSERVE TWO FOXES THAT LIVE IN OUR WOODS. TO LURE THEM HERE, I'VE TIED TWO DEAD CHICKENS TO THAT POST OVER THERE. THEY PREFER FRESH MEAT, BUT THE DEAD BIRDS WILL STIMULATE THEIR SENSE OF SMELL.
TO HAVE THE CHANCE TO SEE THEM, WE MUST FOLLOW THREE RULES. FIRST, WE BLEND INTO THE BACKGROUND-- HUH?
DON'T YOU HAVE A LESS CONSPICUOUS JACKET? TAKE THAT OFF RIGHT NOW!
UH!
NEXT, KEEPING STILL IS ALSO VERY IMPORTANT!
OH, SORRY!
SMACK
I DIDN'T SEE YOU, MISTER!
AND LASTLY, YOU HAVE TO BE SILENT SO THE ANIMALS WON'T BE AFRAID.
NOW HUSH, AND LET'S WAIT!
TOTO, STOP!
UH, I WANTED TO BORROW HIS BINOCULARS TO SEE BETTER... SIR!
NOW, WE HAVE EVERY LIKELIHOOD OF SEEING THE FOXES!
BON Appetit

"The Fifth Element"

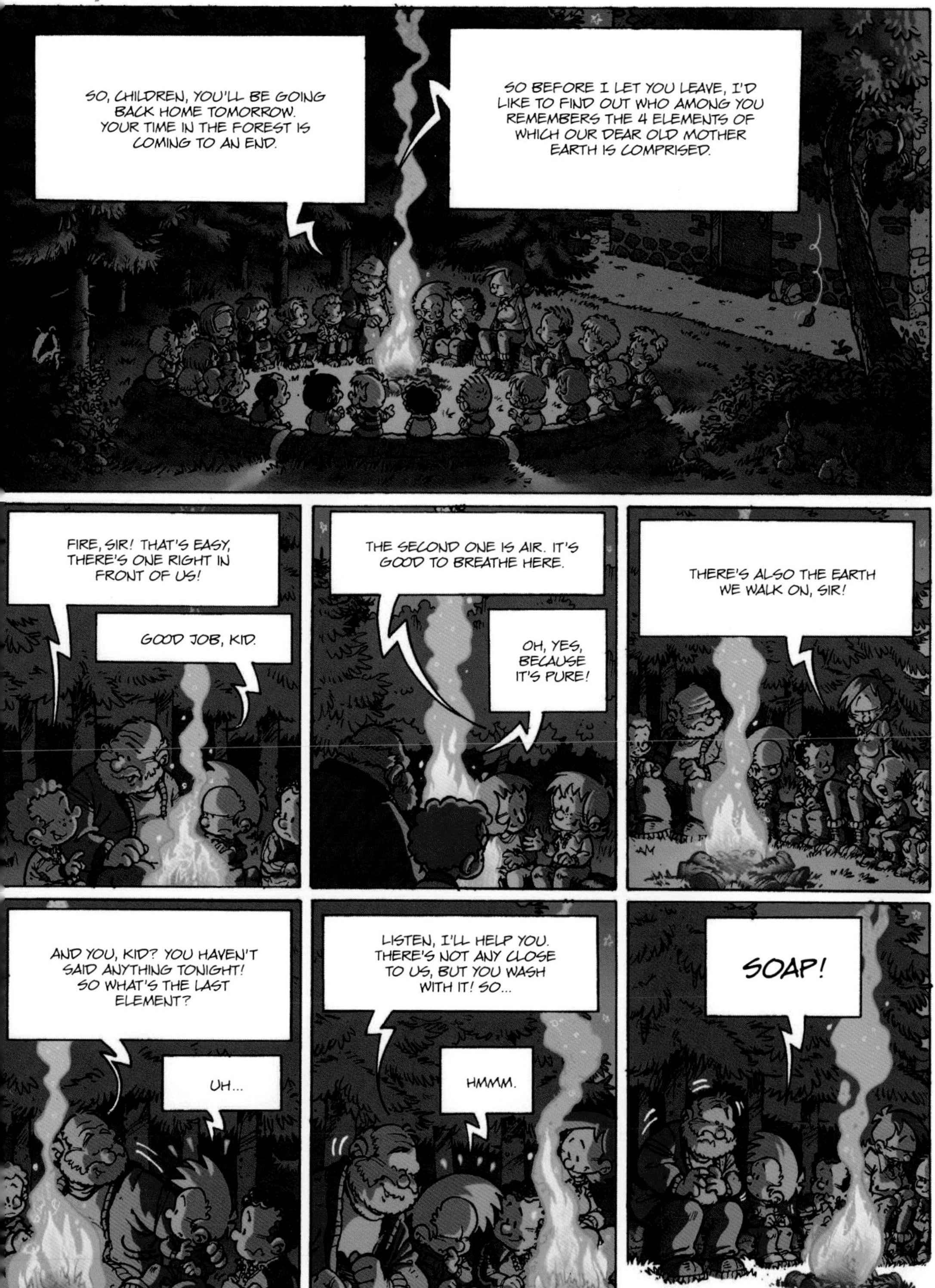
SO, CHILDREN, YOU'LL BE GOING BACK HOME TOMORROW. YOUR TIME IN THE FOREST IS COMING TO AN END.
SO BEFORE I LET YOU LEAVE, I'D LIKE TO FIND OUT WHO AMONG YOU REMEMBERS THE 4 ELEMENTS OF WHICH OUR DEAR OLD MOTHER EARTH IS COMPRISED.
FIRE, SIR! THAT'S EASY, THERE'S ONE RIGHT IN FRONT OF US!
GOOD JOB, KID.
THE SECOND ONE IS AIR. IT'S GOOD TO BREATHE HERE.
OH, YES, BECAUSE IT'S PURE!
THERE'S ALSO THE EARTH WE WALK ON, SIR!
AND YOU, KID? YOU HAVEN'T SAID ANYTHING TONIGHT! SO WHAT'S THE LAST ELEMENT?
UH...
LISTEN, I'LL HELP YOU. THERE'S NOT ANY CLOSE TO US, BUT YOU WASH WITH IT! SO...
HMMM.
SOAP!

"Souvenirs and Forgetfulness"

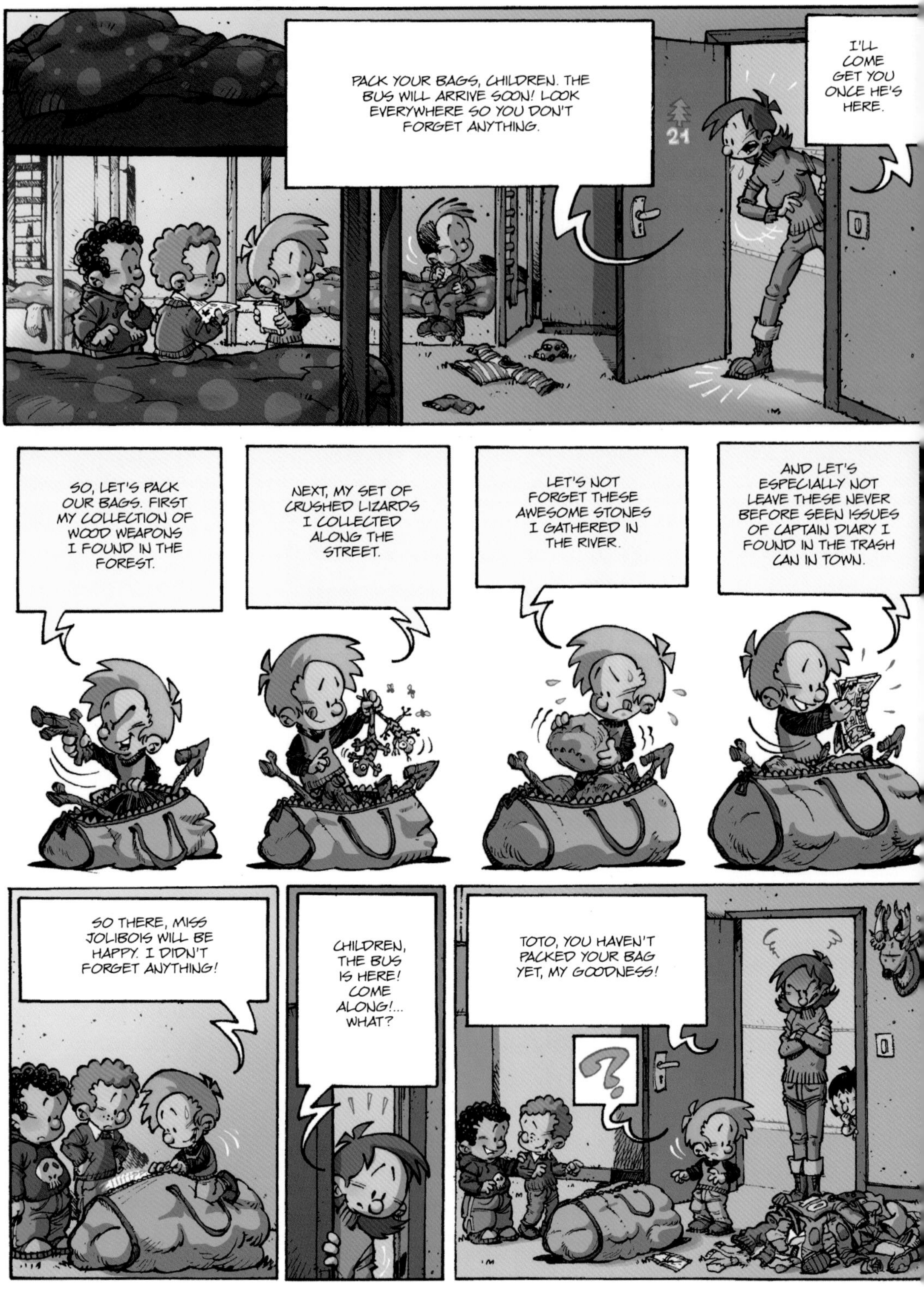
PACK YOUR BAGS, CHILDREN. THE BUS WILL ARRIVE SOON! LOOK EVERYWHERE SO YOU DON'T FORGET ANYTHING.
I'LL COME GET YOU ONCE HE'S HERE.
21
SO, LET'S PACK OUR BAGS. FIRST MY COLLECTION OF WOOD WEAPONS I FOUND IN THE FOREST.
NEXT, MY SET OF CRUSHED LIZARDS I COLLECTED ALONG THE STREET.
LET'S NOT FORGET THESE AWESOME STONES I GATHERED IN THE RIVER.
AND LET'S ESPECIALLY NOT LEAVE THESE NEVER BEFORE SEEN ISSUES OF CAPTAIN DIARY I FOUND IN THE TRASH CAN IN TOWN.
SO THERE, MISS JOLIBOIS WILL BE HAPPY. I DIDN'T FORGET ANYTHING!
CHILDREN, THE BUS IS HERE! COME ALONG!... WHAT?
TOTO, YOU HAVEN'T PACKED YOUR BAG YET, MY GOODNESS!

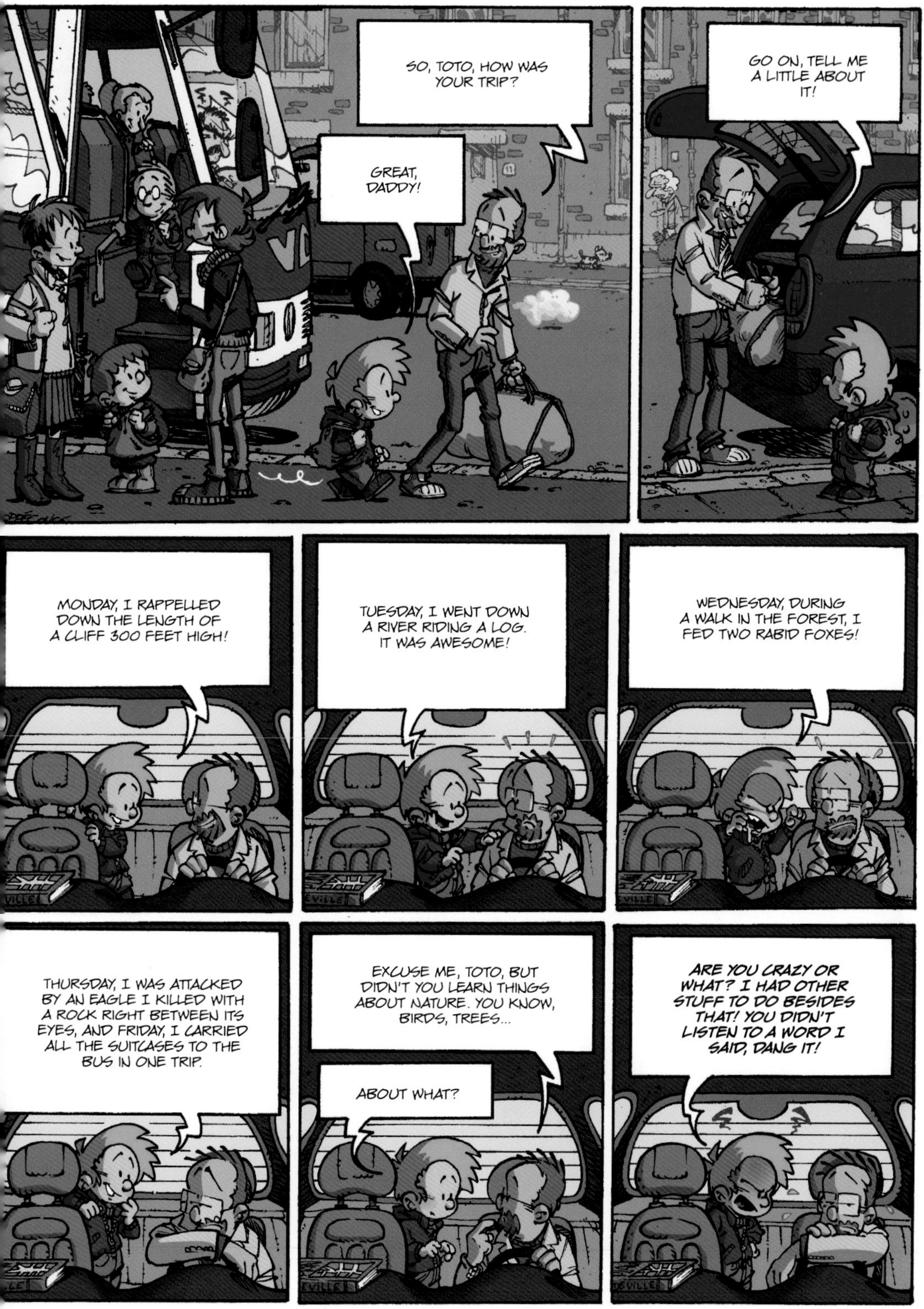
SO, TOTO, HOW WAS YOUR TRIP?
GREAT, DADDY!
GO ON, TELL ME A LITTLE ABOUT IT!
MONDAY, I RAPPELLED DOWN THE LENGTH OF A CLIFF 300 FEET HIGH!
TUESDAY, I WENT DOWN A RIVER RIDING A LOG. IT WAS AWESOME!
WEDNESDAY, DURING A WALK IN THE FOREST, I FED TWO RABID FOXES!
THURSDAY, I WAS ATTACKED BY AN EAGLE I KILLED WITH A ROCK RIGHT BETWEEN ITS EYES, AND FRIDAY, I CARRIED ALL THE SUITCASES TO THE BUS IN ONE TRIP.
EXCUSE ME, TOTO, BUT DIDN'T YOU LEARN THINGS ABOUT NATURE. YOU KNOW, BIRDS, TREES...
ABOUT WHAT?
ARE YOU CRAZY OR WHAT? I HAD OTHER STUFF TO DO BESIDES THAT! YOU DIDN'T LISTEN TO A WORD I SAID, DANG IT!

"An Ounce of Prevention is Worth a Pound of Laughs"

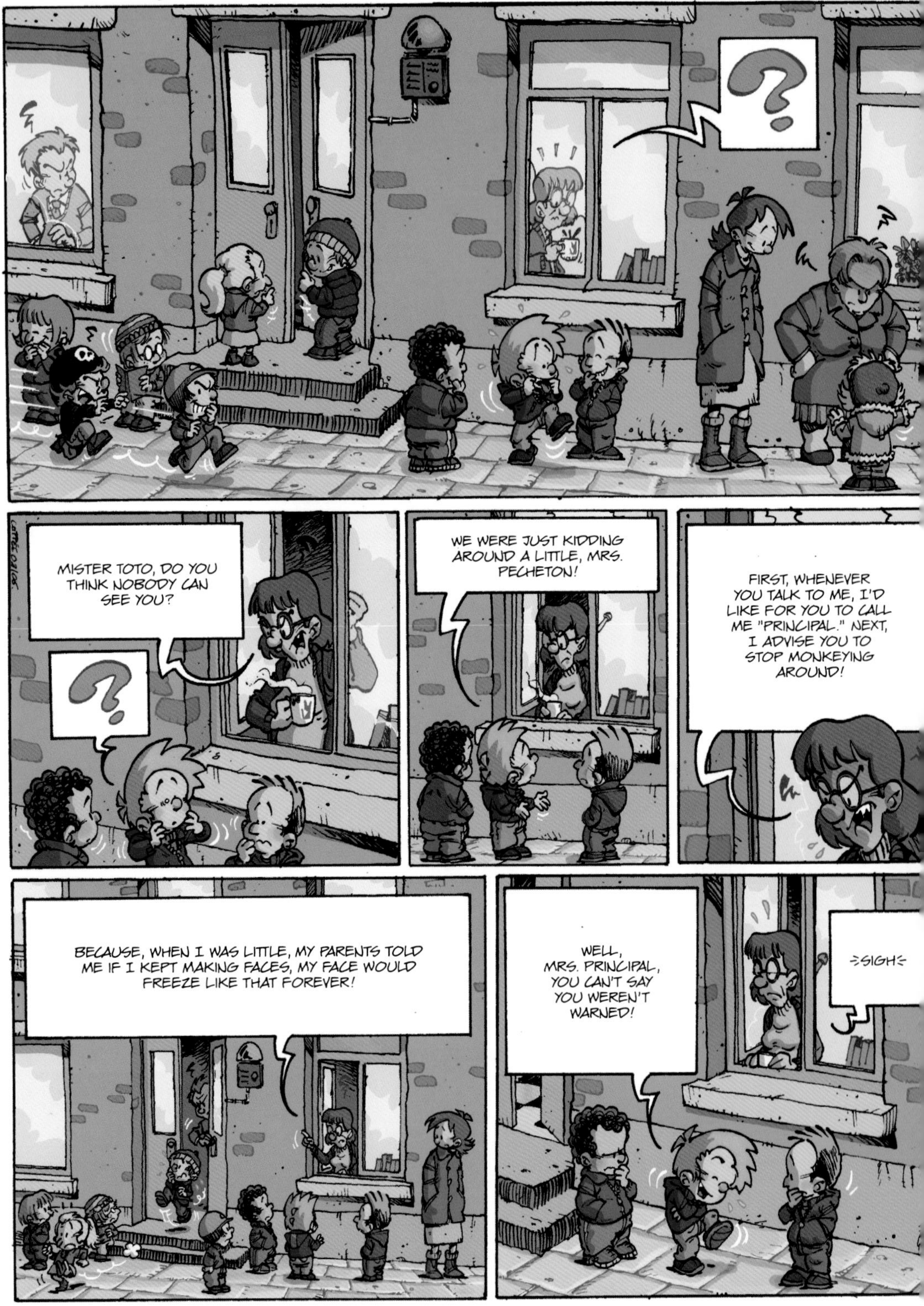
?
MISTER TOTO, DO YOU THINK NOBODY CAN SEE YOU?
?
WE WERE JUST KIDDING AROUND A LITTLE, MRS. PECHETON!
FIRST, WHENEVER YOU TALK TO ME, I'D LIKE FOR YOU TO CALL ME "PRINCIPAL." NEXT, I ADVISE YOU TO STOP MONKEYING AROUND!
BECAUSE, WHEN I WAS LITTLE, MY PARENTS TOLD ME IF I KEPT MAKING FACES, MY FACE WOULD FREEZE LIKE THAT FOREVER!
WELL, MRS. PRINCIPAL, YOU CAN'T SAY YOU WEREN'T WARNED!
SIGH

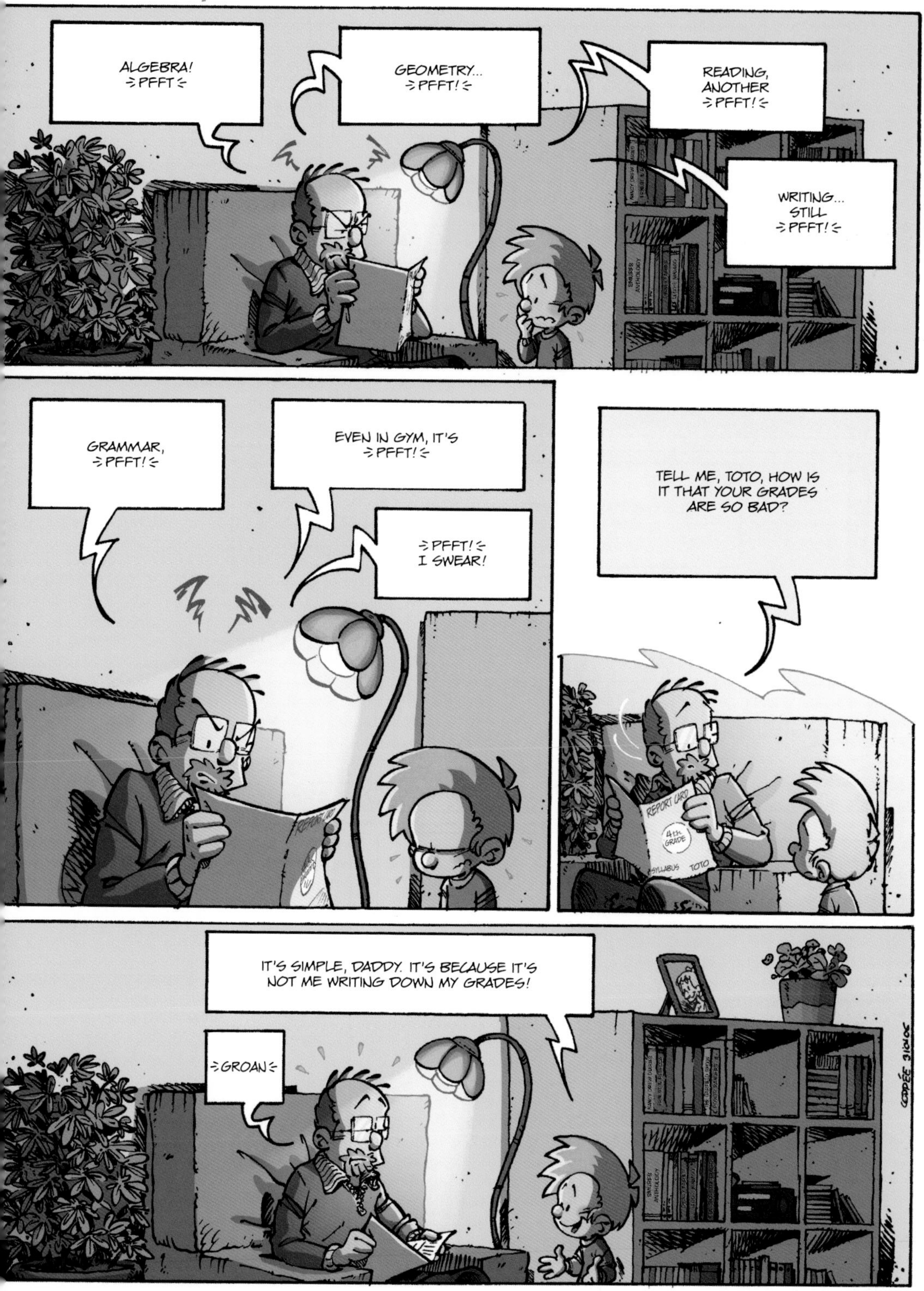
ALGEBRA! ⇉PFFT⇇
GEOMETRY... ⇉PFFT!⇇
READING, ANOTHER ⇉PFFT!⇇
WRITING... STILL ⇉PFFT!⇇
GRAMMAR, ⇉PFFT!⇇
EVEN IN GYM, IT'S ⇉PFFT!⇇
⇉PFFT!⇇ I SWEAR!
TELL ME, TOTO, HOW IS IT THAT YOUR GRADES ARE SO BAD?
REPORT CARD
4th GRADE
SYLLABUS
TOTO
IT'S SIMPLE, DADDY. IT'S BECAUSE IT'S NOT ME WRITING DOWN MY GRADES!
⇉GROAN⇇

"Snow Falls"

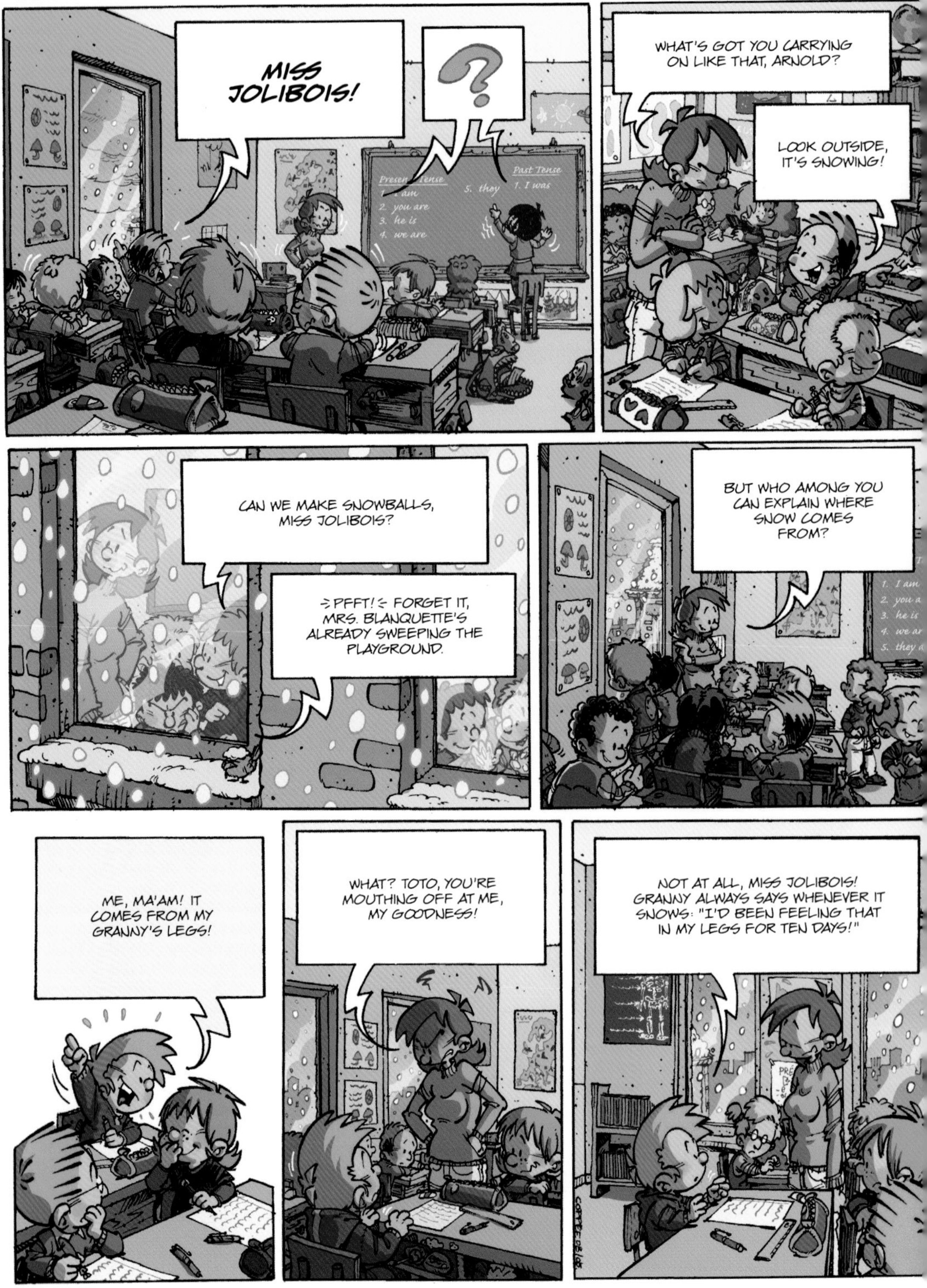

MISS JOLIBOIS!
?
Present Tense
1. I am
2. you are
3. he is
4. we are
5. they
Past Tense
1. I was
WHAT'S GOT YOU CARRYING ON LIKE THAT, ARNOLD?
LOOK OUTSIDE, IT'S SNOWING!
CAN WE MAKE SNOWBALLS, MISS JOLIBOIS?
PFFT! FORGET IT, MRS. BLANQUETTE'S ALREADY SWEEPING THE PLAYGROUND.
BUT WHO AMONG YOU CAN EXPLAIN WHERE SNOW COMES FROM?
ME, MA'AM! IT COMES FROM MY GRANNY'S LEGS!
WHAT? TOTO, YOU'RE MOUTHING OFF AT ME, MY GOODNESS!
NOT AT ALL, MISS JOLIBOIS! GRANNY ALWAYS SAYS WHENEVER IT SNOWS: "I'D BEEN FEELING THAT IN MY LEGS FOR TEN DAYS!"

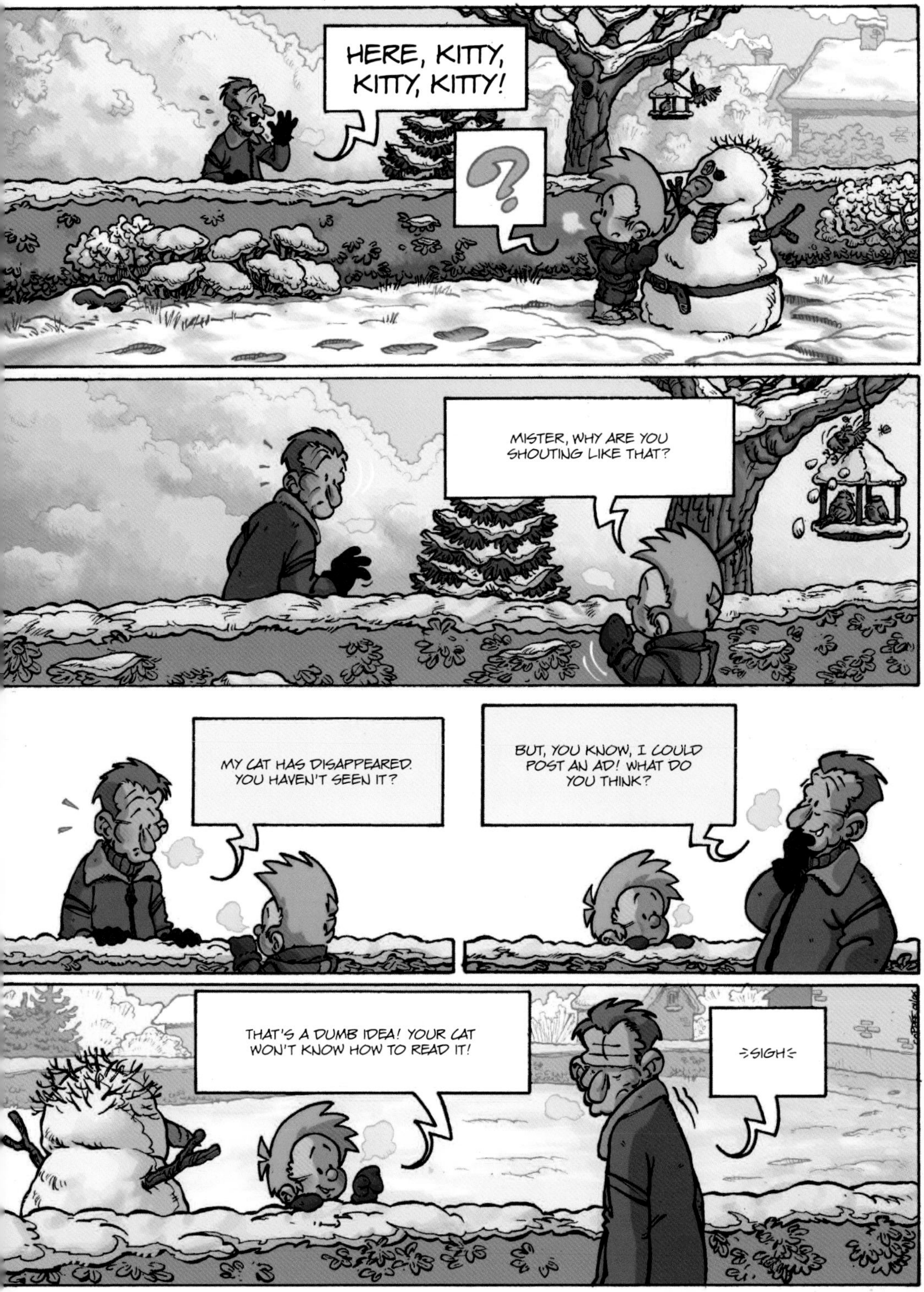
HERE, KITTY, KITTY, KITTY!
?
MISTER, WHY ARE YOU SHOUTING LIKE THAT?
MY CAT HAS DISAPPEARED. YOU HAVEN'T SEEN IT?
BUT, YOU KNOW, I COULD POST AN AD! WHAT DO YOU THINK?
THAT'S A DUMB IDEA! YOUR CAT WON'T KNOW HOW TO READ IT!
=SIGH=

"In Search of Lost Cats" (Part II)

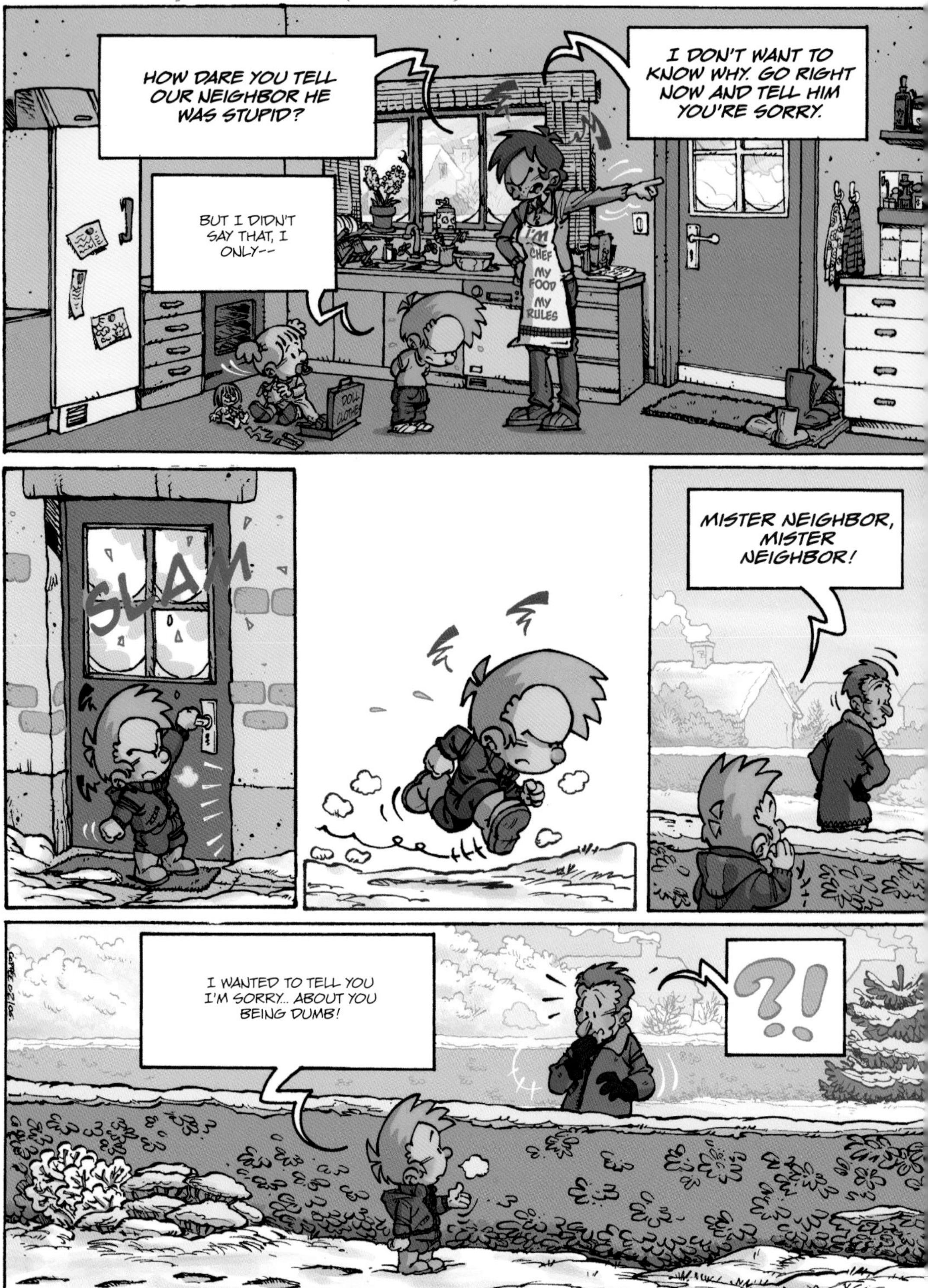
HOW DARE YOU TELL OUR NEIGHBOR HE WAS STUPID?
BUT I DIDN'T SAY THAT, I ONLY--
I DON'T WANT TO KNOW WHY. GO RIGHT NOW AND TELL HIM YOU'RE SORRY.
I'M CHEF MY FOOD MY RULES
DOLL CLOTHES
SLAM
MISTER NEIGHBOR, MISTER NEIGHBOR!
I WANTED TO TELL YOU I'M SORRY... ABOUT YOU BEING DUMB!
?!

"Taste Tests"

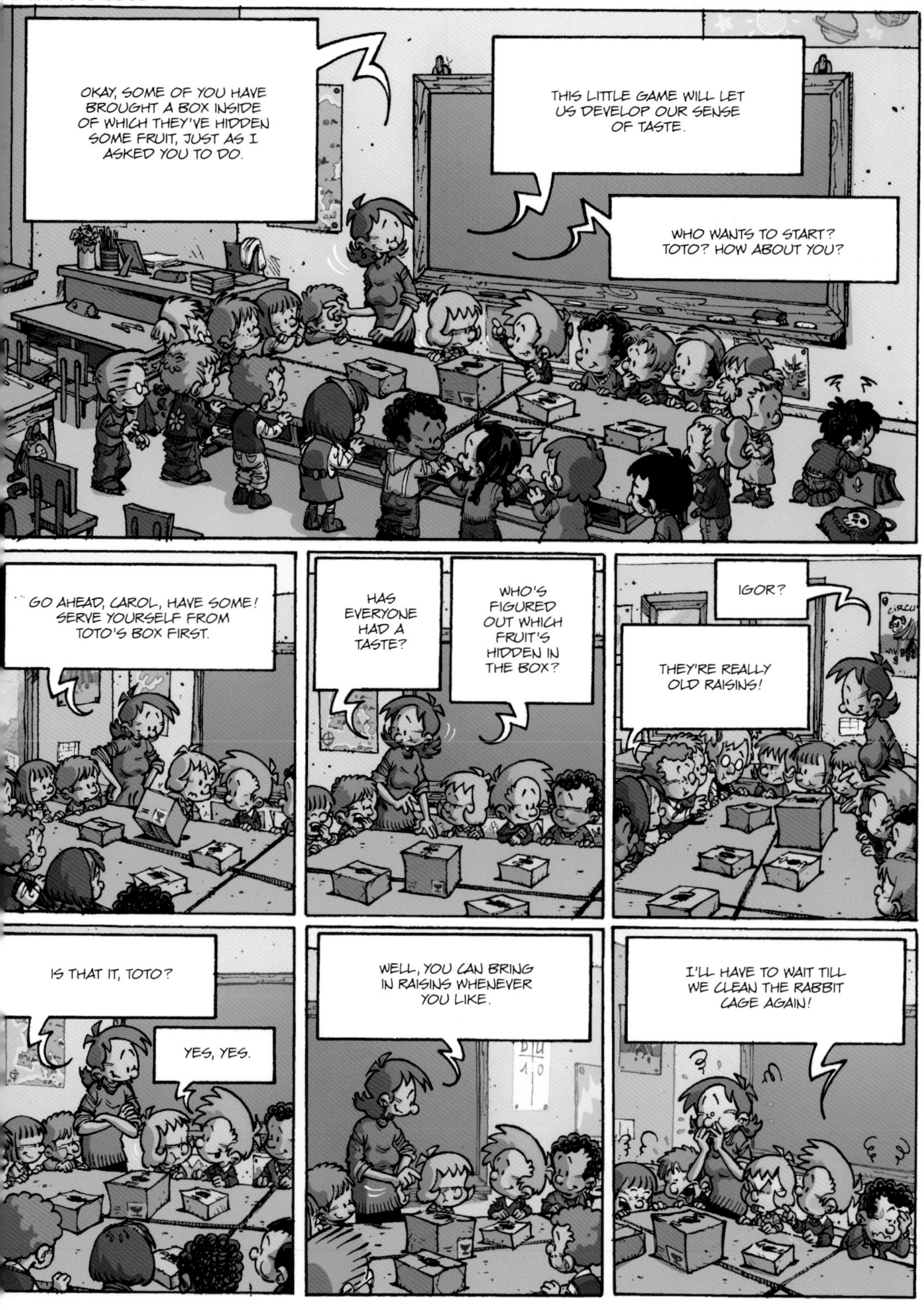
OKAY, SOME OF YOU HAVE BROUGHT A BOX INSIDE OF WHICH THEY'VE HIDDEN SOME FRUIT, JUST AS I ASKED YOU TO DO.
THIS LITTLE GAME WILL LET US DEVELOP OUR SENSE OF TASTE.
WHO WANTS TO START? TOTO? HOW ABOUT YOU?
GO AHEAD, CAROL, HAVE SOME! SERVE YOURSELF FROM TOTO'S BOX FIRST.
HAS EVERYONE HAD A TASTE?
WHO'S FIGURED OUT WHICH FRUIT'S HIDDEN IN THE BOX?
IGOR?
THEY'RE REALLY OLD RAISINS!
IS THAT IT, TOTO?
YES, YES.
WELL, YOU CAN BRING IN RAISINS WHENEVER YOU LIKE.
I'LL HAVE TO WAIT TILL WE CLEAN THE RABBIT CAGE AGAIN!

"Zeroes Across the Board"

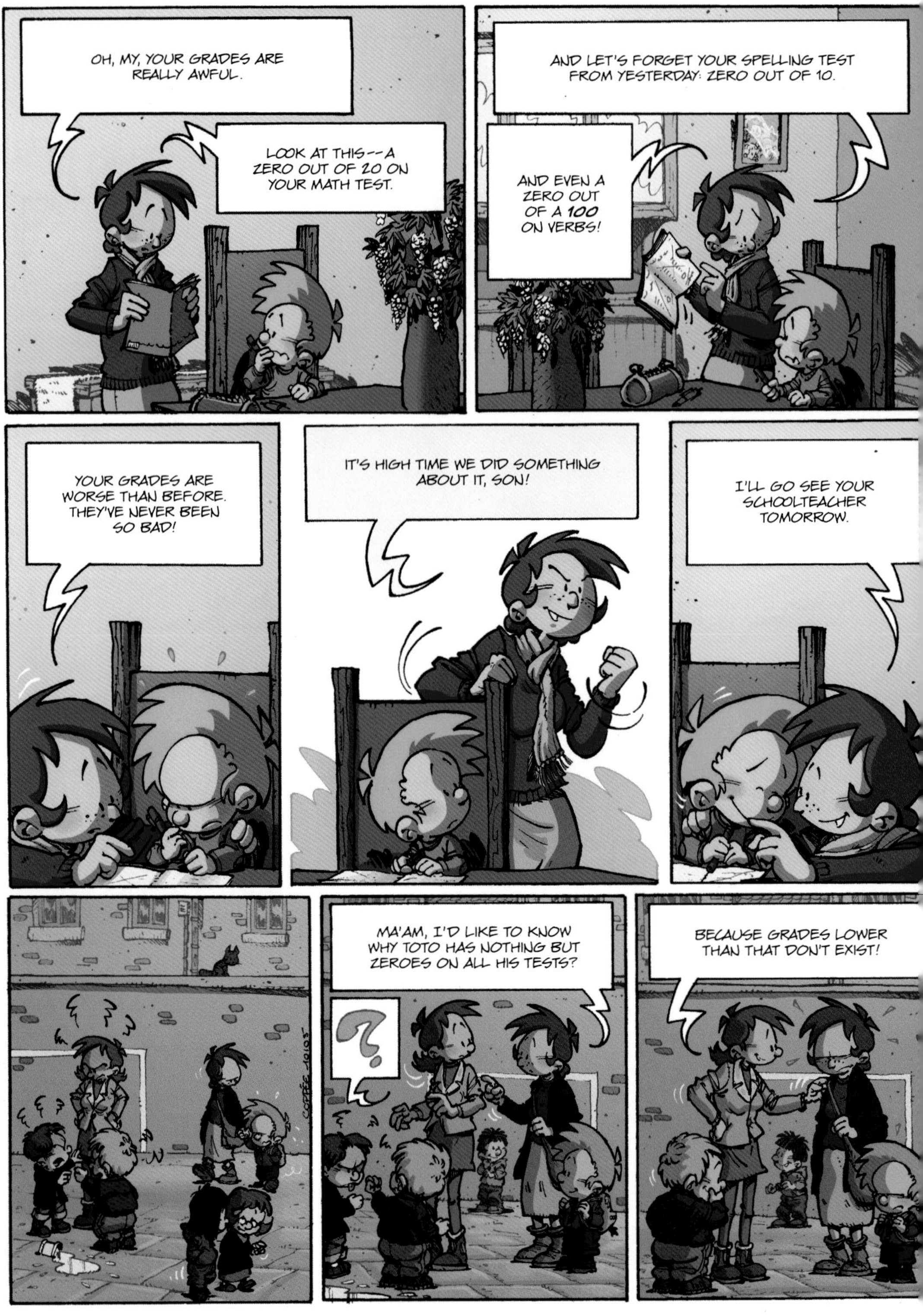
OH, MY, YOUR GRADES ARE REALLY AWFUL.
LOOK AT THIS--A ZERO OUT OF 20 ON YOUR MATH TEST.
AND LET'S FORGET YOUR SPELLING TEST FROM YESTERDAY: ZERO OUT OF 10.
AND EVEN A ZERO OUT OF A 100 ON VERBS!
YOUR GRADES ARE WORSE THAN BEFORE. THEY'VE NEVER BEEN SO BAD!
IT'S HIGH TIME WE DID SOMETHING ABOUT IT, SON!
I'LL GO SEE YOUR SCHOOLTEACHER TOMORROW.
MA'AM, I'D LIKE TO KNOW WHY TOTO HAS NOTHING BUT ZEROES ON ALL HIS TESTS?
?
BECAUSE GRADES LOWER THAN THAT DON'T EXIST!

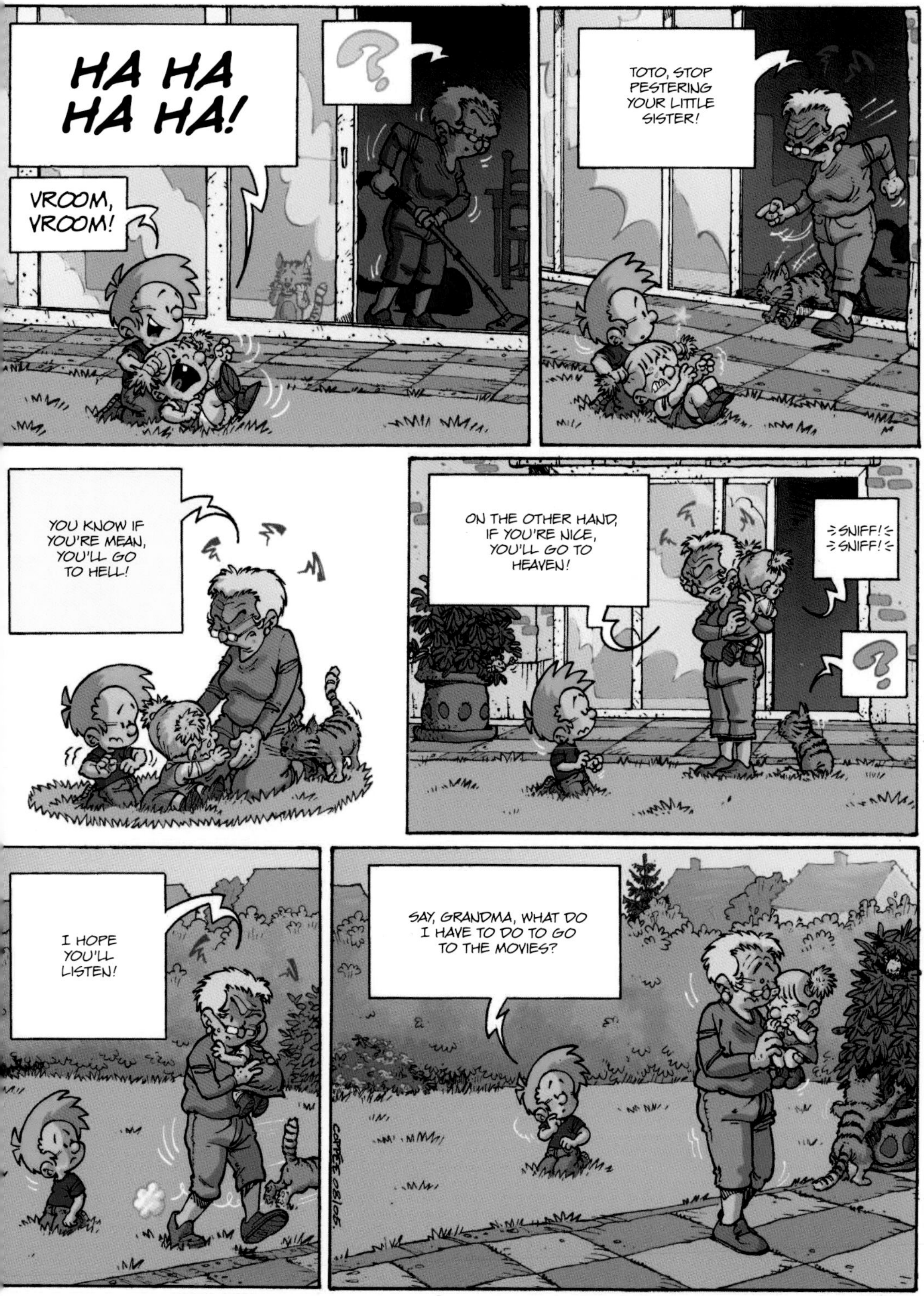
HA HA
HA HA!
VROOM, VROOM!
?
TOTO, STOP PESTERING YOUR LITTLE SISTER!
YOU KNOW IF YOU'RE MEAN, YOU'LL GO TO HELL!
ON THE OTHER HAND, IF YOU'RE NICE, YOU'LL GO TO HEAVEN!
SNIFF! SNIFF!
?
I HOPE YOU'LL LISTEN!
SAY, GRANDMA, WHAT DO I HAVE TO DO TO GO TO THE MOVIES?

SO THE FIRST LITTLE PIG LEFT TO GO BUILD HIS HOUSE...

...ON THE WAY, HE MET A MAN LABORIOUSLY PUSHING A WHEEL-BARROW FULL OF STRAW.

THE PIG APPROACHED THE MAN AND SAID:

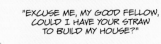

"EXCUSE ME, MY GOOD FELLOW, COULD I HAVE YOUR STRAW TO BUILD MY HOUSE?"

AND, CHILDREN, WHAT DO YOU THINK WAS THE PEASANT'S RESPONSE?

I KNOW, I KNOW!

AH, YES, TOTO, AND WHAT DO YOU THINK HE SAID?

"HOLY SHNIKIES, THAT'S A TALKING A PIG!"

"It's All in Your Head"

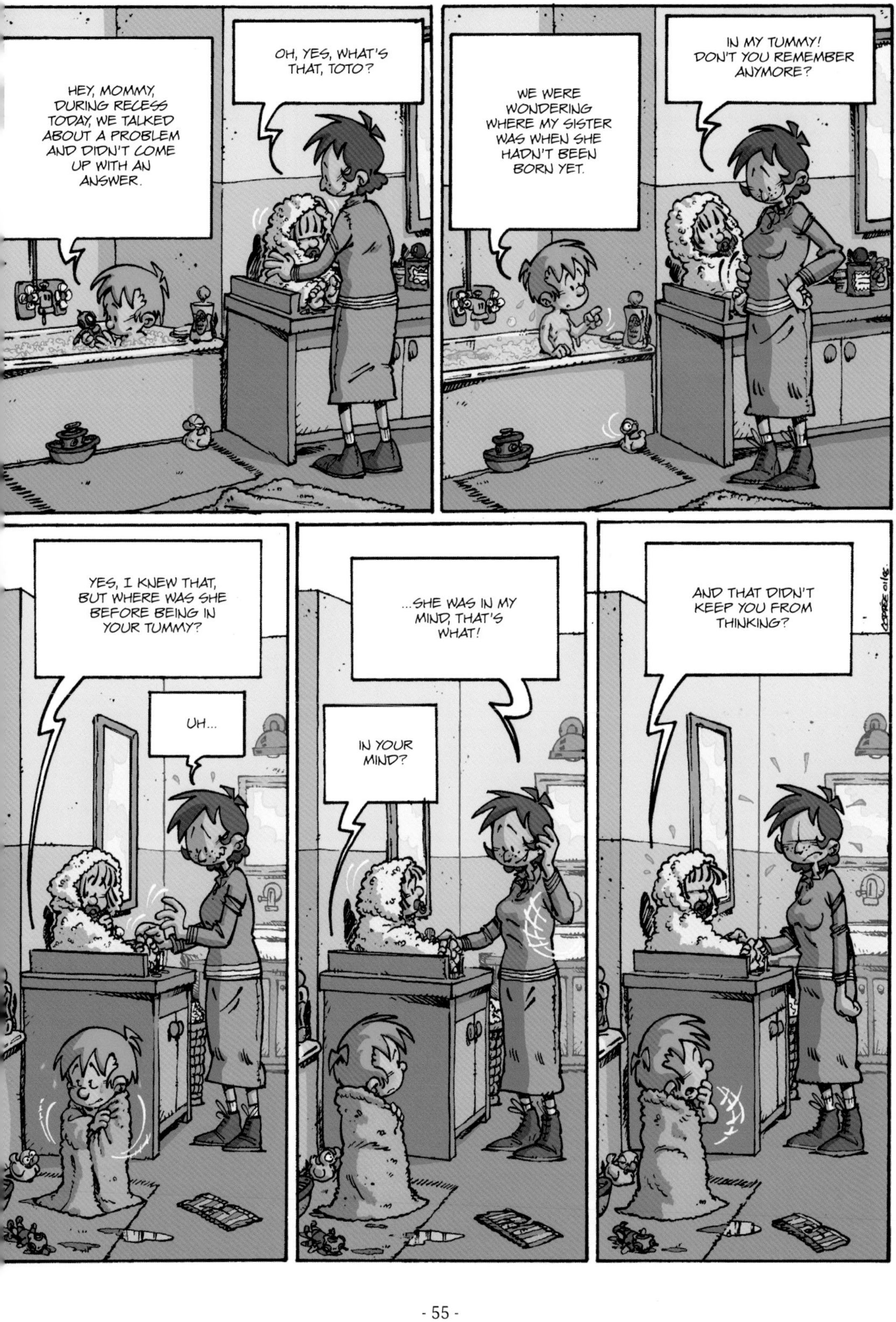
HEY, MOMMY, DURING RECESS TODAY, WE TALKED ABOUT A PROBLEM AND DIDN'T COME UP WITH AN ANSWER.
OH, YES, WHAT'S THAT, TOTO?
WE WERE WONDERING WHERE MY SISTER WAS WHEN SHE HADN'T BEEN BORN YET.
IN MY TUMMY! DON'T YOU REMEMBER ANYMORE?
YES, I KNEW THAT, BUT WHERE WAS SHE BEFORE BEING IN YOUR TUMMY?
UH...
IN YOUR MIND?
...SHE WAS IN MY MIND, THAT'S WHAT!
AND THAT DIDN'T KEEP YOU FROM THINKING?

"The Day for Problems"

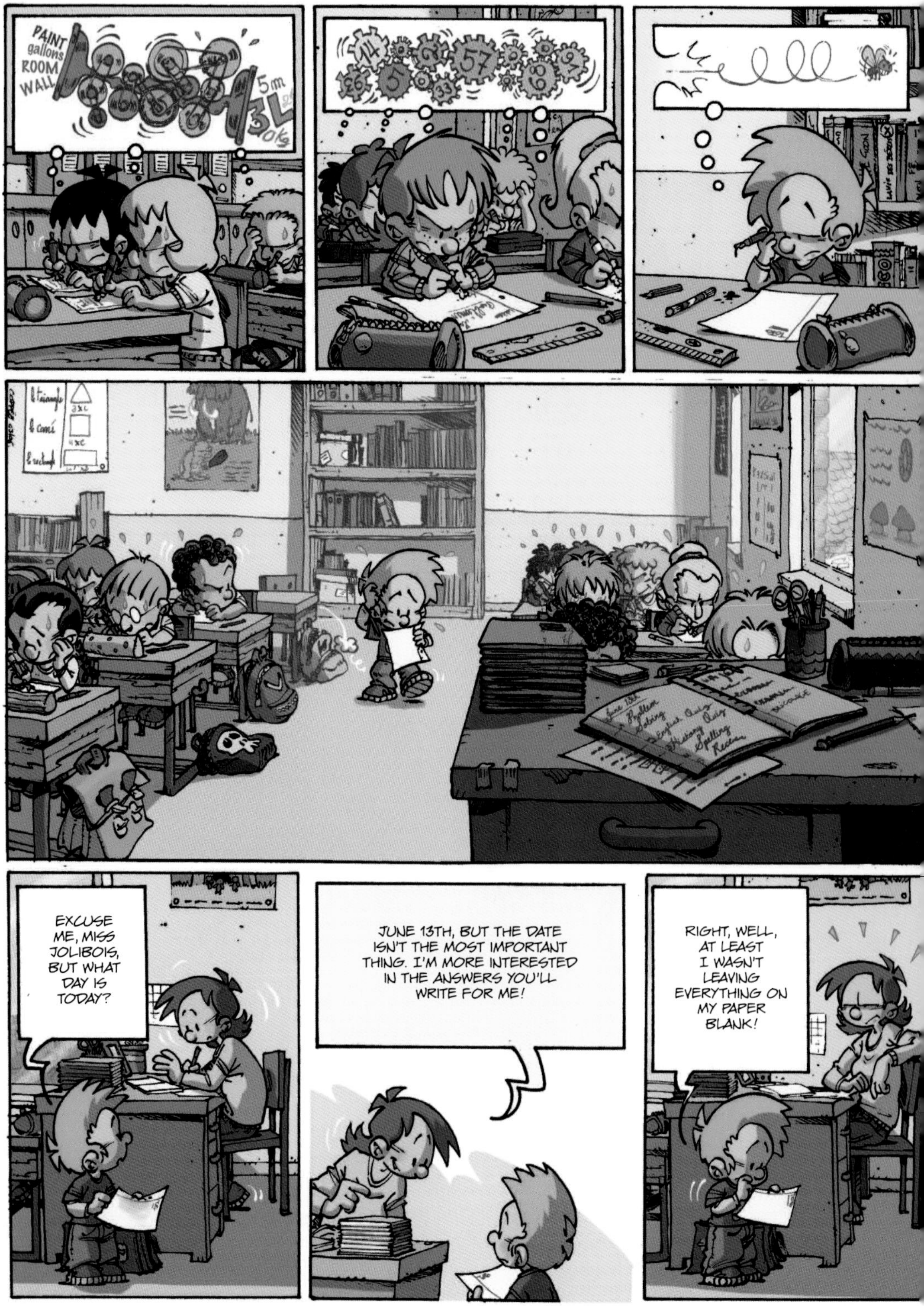

PAINT
gallons
ROOM
WALL
5m
3L
EXCUSE ME, MISS JOLIBOIS, BUT WHAT DAY IS TODAY?
JUNE 13TH, BUT THE DATE ISN'T THE MOST IMPORTANT THING. I'M MORE INTERESTED IN THE ANSWERS YOU'LL WRITE FOR ME!
RIGHT, WELL, AT LEAST I WASN'T LEAVING EVERYTHING ON MY PAPER BLANK!

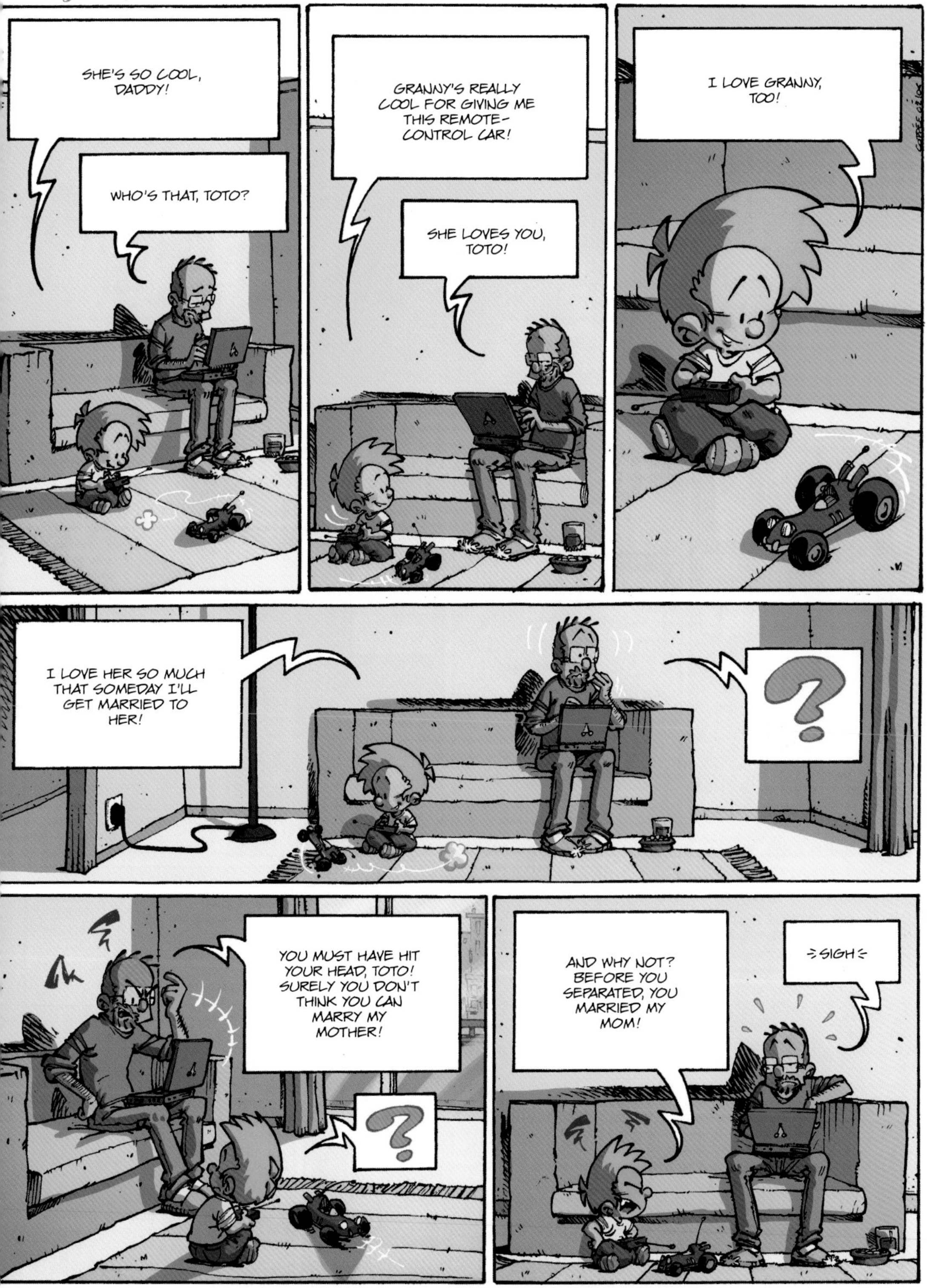
SHE'S SO COOL, DADDY!
WHO'S THAT, TOTO?
GRANNY'S REALLY COOL FOR GIVING ME THIS REMOTE-CONTROL CAR!
SHE LOVES YOU, TOTO!
I LOVE GRANNY, TOO!
I LOVE HER SO MUCH THAT SOMEDAY I'LL GET MARRIED TO HER!
?
YOU MUST HAVE HIT YOUR HEAD, TOTO! SURELY YOU DON'T THINK YOU CAN MARRY MY MOTHER!
?
AND WHY NOT? BEFORE YOU SEPARATED, YOU MARRIED MY MOM!
SIGH

"Family Ties"

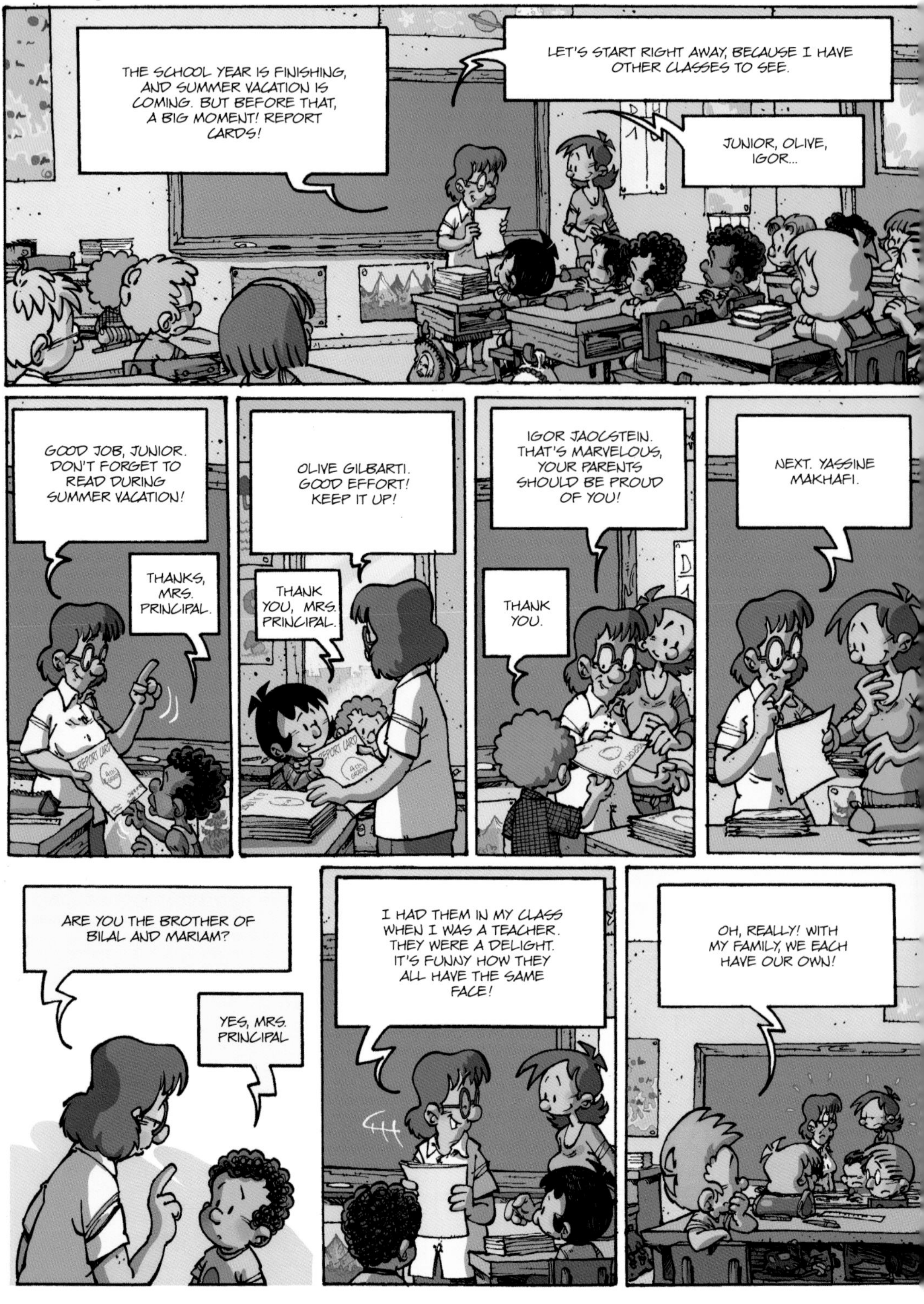
THE SCHOOL YEAR IS FINISHING, AND SUMMER VACATION IS COMING. BUT BEFORE THAT, A BIG MOMENT! REPORT CARDS!
LET'S START RIGHT AWAY, BECAUSE I HAVE OTHER CLASSES TO SEE.
JUNIOR, OLIVE, IGOR...
GOOD JOB, JUNIOR. DON'T FORGET TO READ DURING SUMMER VACATION!
THANKS, MRS. PRINCIPAL.
OLIVE GILBARTI. GOOD EFFORT! KEEP IT UP!
THANK YOU, MRS. PRINCIPAL.
IGOR JAOCSTEIN. THAT'S MARVELOUS, YOUR PARENTS SHOULD BE PROUD OF YOU!
THANK YOU.
NEXT. YASSINE MAKHAFI.
ARE YOU THE BROTHER OF BILAL AND MARIAM?
YES, MRS. PRINCIPAL
I HAD THEM IN MY CLASS WHEN I WAS A TEACHER. THEY WERE A DELIGHT. IT'S FUNNY HOW THEY ALL HAVE THE SAME FACE!
OH, REALLY! WITH MY FAMILY, WE EACH HAVE OUR OWN!

"Good Parents and Bad Grades"

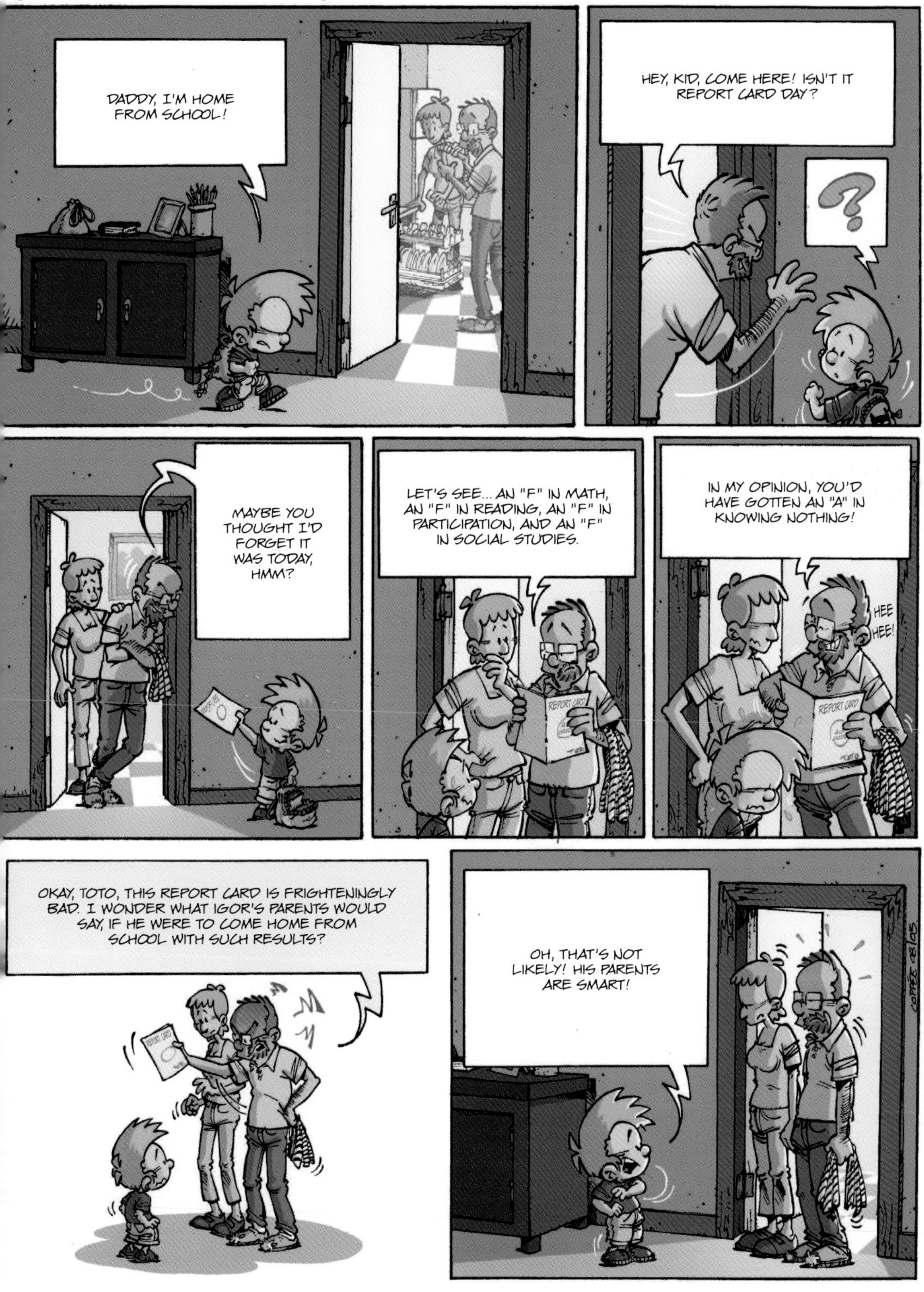

DADDY, I'M HOME FROM SCHOOL!
HEY, KID, COME HERE! ISN'T IT REPORT CARD DAY?
?
MAYBE YOU THOUGHT I'D FORGET IT WAS TODAY, HMM?
REPORT CARD
LET'S SEE... AN "F" IN MATH, AN "F" IN READING, AN "F" IN PARTICIPATION, AND AN "F" IN SOCIAL STUDIES.
REPORT CARD
IN MY OPINION, YOU'D HAVE GOTTEN AN "A" IN KNOWING NOTHING!
HEE HEE!
REPORT CARD
OKAY, TOTO, THIS REPORT CARD IS FRIGHTENINGLY BAD. I WONDER WHAT IGOR'S PARENTS WOULD SAY, IF HE WERE TO COME HOME FROM SCHOOL WITH SUCH RESULTS?
REPORT CARD
OH, THAT'S NOT LIKELY! HIS PARENTS ARE SMART!

"Chicken Talk"

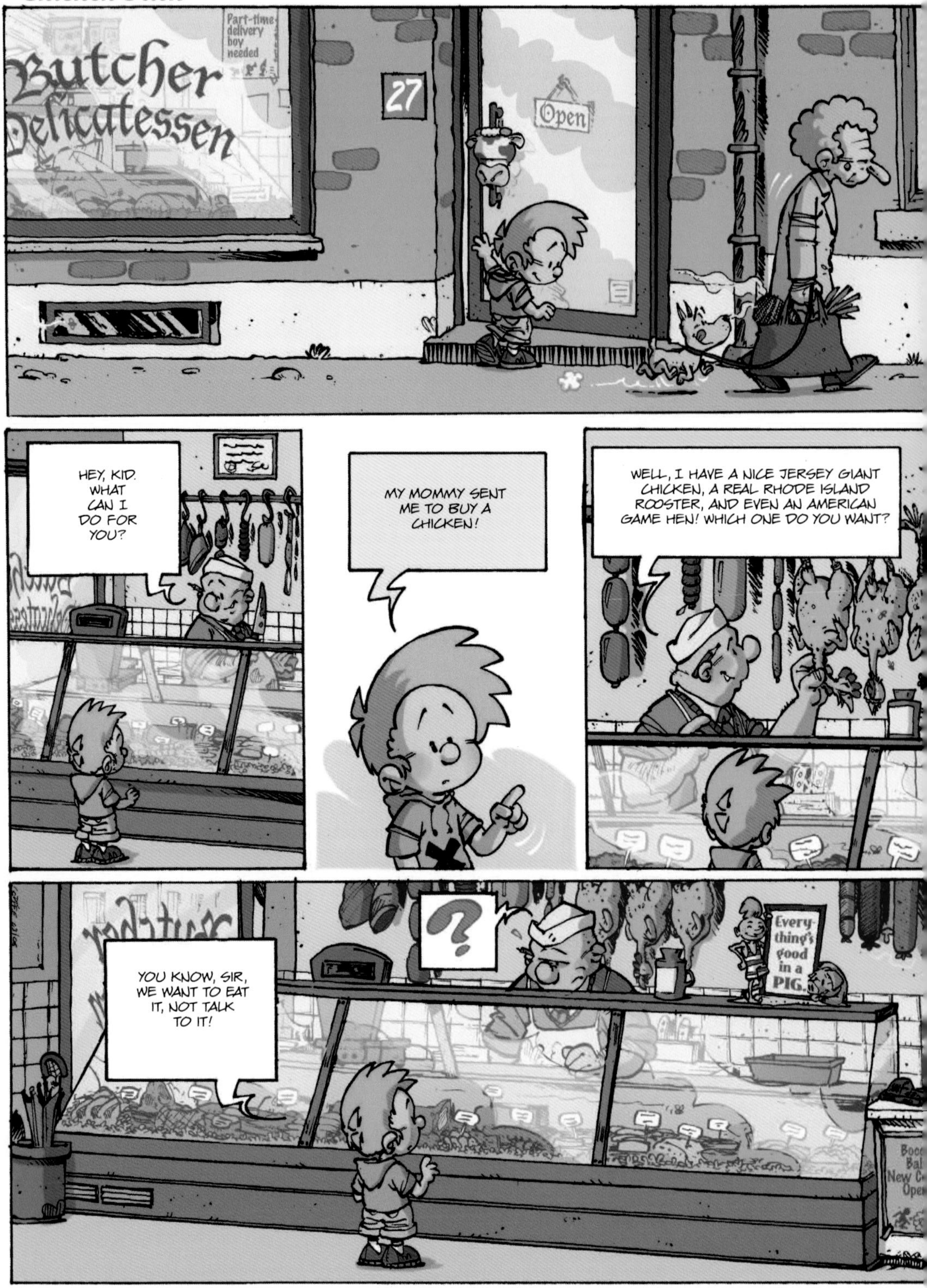
Part-time delivery boy needed
Butcher Delicatessen
27
Open
HEY, KID. WHAT CAN I DO FOR YOU?
MY MOMMY SENT ME TO BUY A CHICKEN!
WELL, I HAVE A NICE JERSEY GIANT CHICKEN, A REAL RHODE ISLAND ROOSTER, AND EVEN AN AMERICAN GAME HEN! WHICH ONE DO YOU WANT?
?
YOU KNOW, SIR, WE WANT TO EAT IT, NOT TALK TO IT!
Every-thing's good in a PIG.

"Generous Idea"

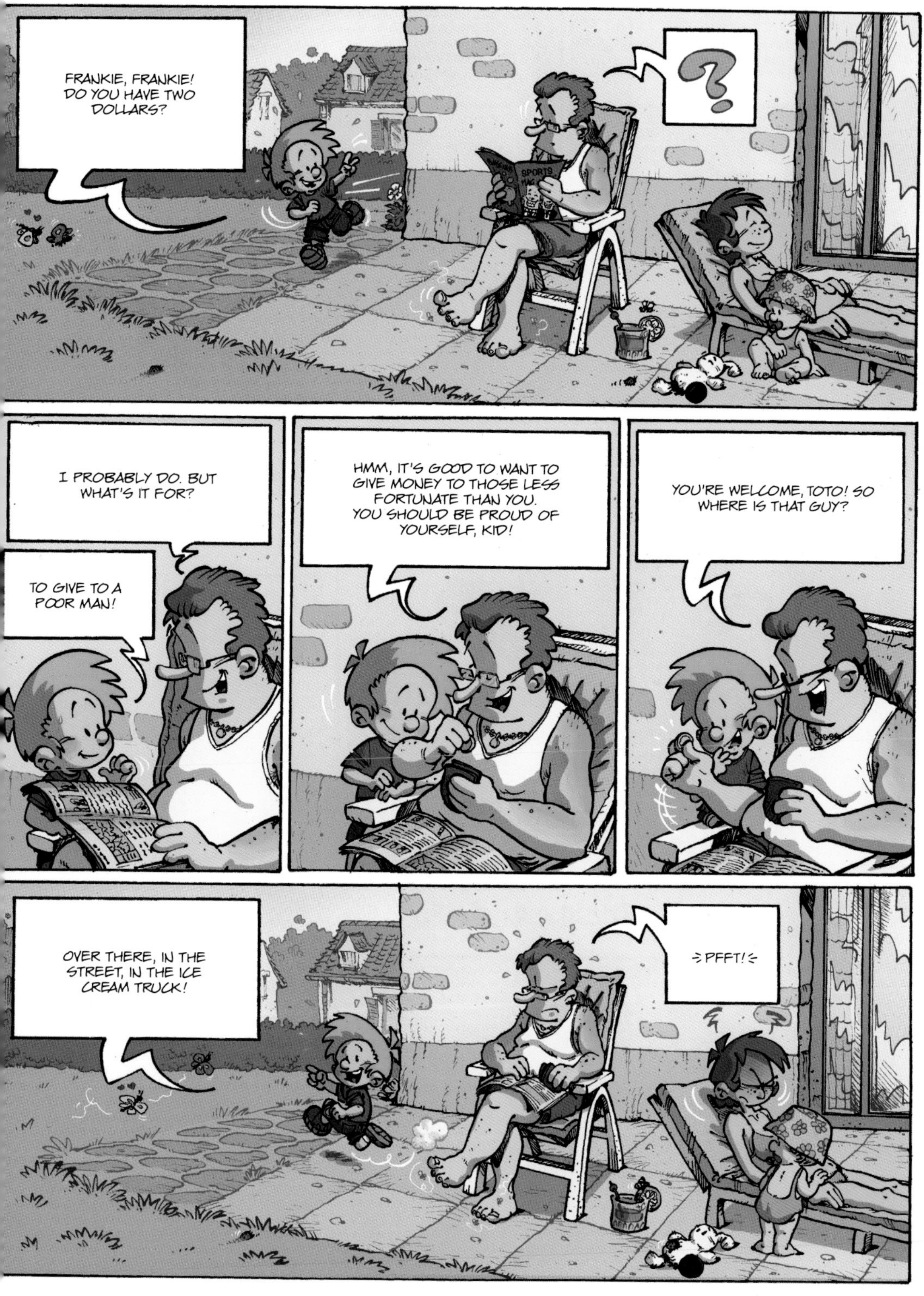
FRANKIE, FRANKIE! DO YOU HAVE TWO DOLLARS?
?
SPORTS MAG
I PROBABLY DO. BUT WHAT'S IT FOR?
TO GIVE TO A POOR MAN!
HMM, IT'S GOOD TO WANT TO GIVE MONEY TO THOSE LESS FORTUNATE THAN YOU. YOU SHOULD BE PROUD OF YOURSELF, KID!
YOU'RE WELCOME, TOTO! SO WHERE IS THAT GUY?
OVER THERE, IN THE STREET, IN THE ICE CREAM TRUCK!
PFFT!

“Question for a Champion (second go-around)”

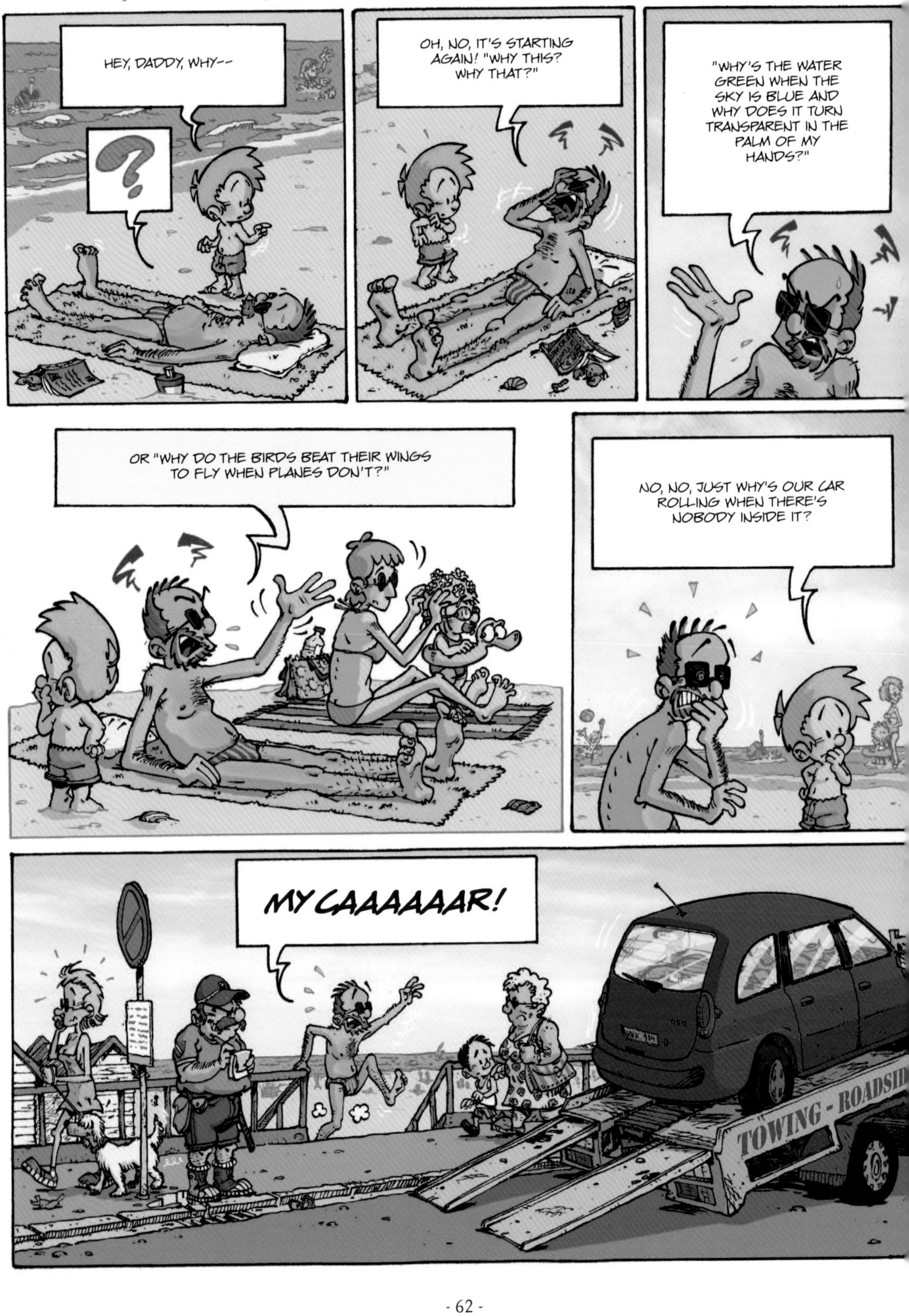
HEY, DADDY, WHY--
OH, NO, IT'S STARTING AGAIN! "WHY THIS? WHY THAT?"
"WHY'S THE WATER GREEN WHEN THE SKY IS BLUE AND WHY DOES IT TURN TRANSPARENT IN THE PALM OF MY HANDS?"
OR "WHY DO THE BIRDS BEAT THEIR WINGS TO FLY WHEN PLANES DON'T?"
NO, NO, JUST WHY'S OUR CAR ROLLING WHEN THERE'S NOBODY INSIDE IT?
MY CAAAAAAR!
TOWING - ROADSID

WATCH OUT FOR PAPERCUTZ™

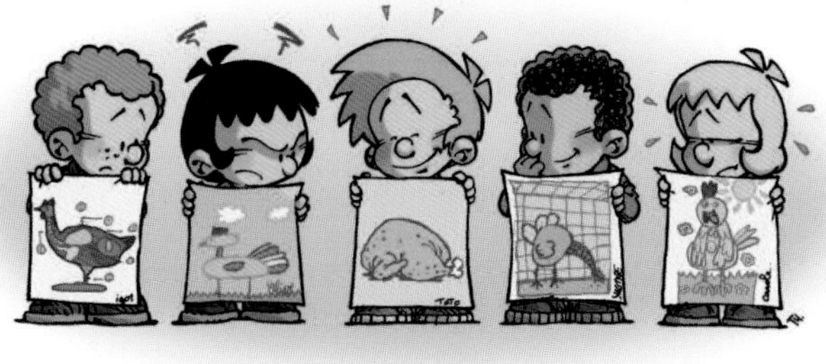

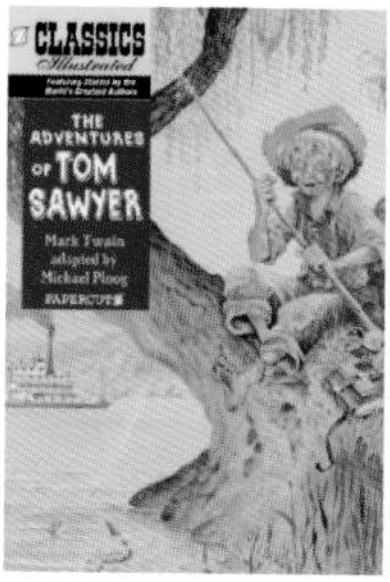
CLASSICS Illustrated
THE ADVENTURES OF TOM SAWYER
Mark Twain
adapted by
Michael Ploog
PAPERCUTZ
CLASSICS ILLUSTRATED © First Classics, Inc.

/elcome to the snarky, somewhat-stupid second TOTO TROUBLE graphic novel by Thierry ppée from Papercutz, that itty-bitty company that's dedicated to publishing great graphic vels for all ages. I'm Jim Salicrup, your bleary-eyed Editor-in-Chief who, like Papercutz, ows where the boys (and one girl) are...

hey say boys will be boys, and we at Papercutz have published a lot of comics to back t up! It didn't all begin with *Bart Simpson* and *Calvin* (from *Calvin and Hobbes*), or n *Bazooka Joe*. There have been tales of bad boys for as long as tales have been told. haps one of the greatest novels ever written about a boy's life has to be *The Adventures Tom Sawyer* by Mark Twain. We like it so much we've published two different comics aptations—one in manga-style by Jean David Morvan, Frederique Voulyze, and Severine evre in CLASSICS ILLUSTRATED DELUXE #4 and one adapted by the great American nics artist Mike Ploog in CLASSICS ILLUSTRATED #19. Both versions are great at capturing spirit of those two adventurous boys, Tom Sawyer and Huckleberry Finn. Yeah, we know y may force you to read the prose novel in school, but despite that, it actually is a great story.

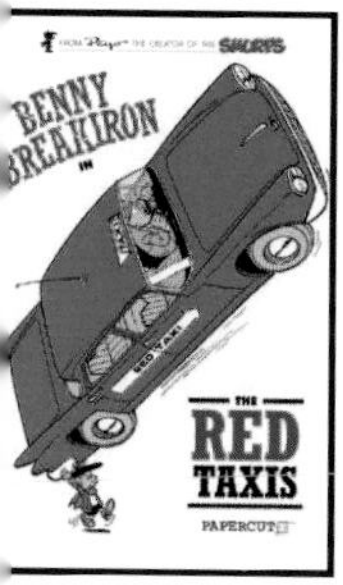
BENNY BREAKIRON
in
THE RED TAXIS
PAPERCUTZ

Speaking of adventure, Papercutz also publishes BENNY BREAKIRON, the story of a French boy who is super-strong, except when he gets a cold. Benny is written and drawn by the creator of THE SMURFS, yet his adventures couldn't be more action-packed. That doesn't mean Benny is like every other super-hero. He's very much a good little boy, yet there are a few mysteries surrounding him—such as where are his parents? How did he get so strong? And why does he hang around with an old cab driver? This is definitely a series worth checking out! (Literally, if they have it at the library!)

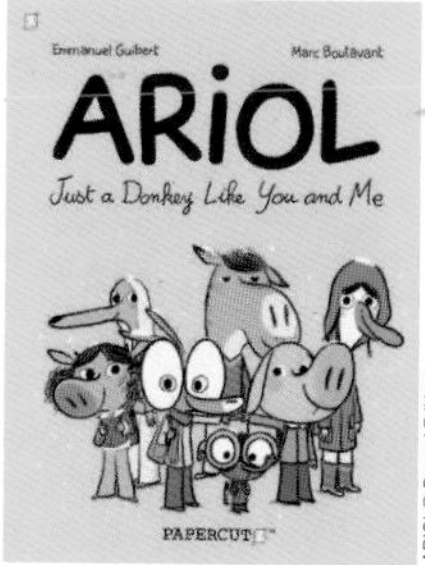
Emmanuel Guibert
Marc Boutavant
ARiOL
Just a Donkey Like You and Me
PAPERCUTZ
ARIOL© Bayard Editions.

Oddly enough, the most believable graphic novel bad boy series published by Papercutz is about a boy who just happens to be a blue donkey, and his best friend is a pig, and he's hopelessly in love with a cow. Yes, I'm talking about ARIOL by Emmanuel Guibert and Marc Boutavant. Each volume features a collection of ten-page stories that cover every aspect of Ariol's life—at school, at home, on vacation, etc. ol is just a donkey like you or me—he even loves comics, especially *Thunder Horse*. I must n you, once you pick up one ARIOL graphic novel, and enter Ariol's world, you'll love it so ch that you're going to want to collect them all!

nally, there's ERNEST & REBECCA, the graphic novel series by Guillaume Bianco and onello Dalena. Ernest isn't a boy, he's a microbe, actually, and Rebecca is a little six-and-a- f year old girl. So, why am I mentioning them when writing about bad boys? Because in her n way she may be the baddest one of all. When offered membership in the "Buddy Trio"), which consists of tomboy Chris, and boys Diego and Ronald, Rebecca sails through the initiation challenges quite rtlessly! Life, on the other hand, may present bigger challenges--her parents are breaking up, her older sister ignores and she's sick a lot. But Rebecca is so full of life there's never a dull moment. And the writing and artwork are so nderful, you'll want to savor every page.

hich brings us back to TOTO TROUBLE. At first glance this series may appear to be nothing more than dumb s—and there's nothing wrong with that. But if you look a little closer, you may find that there's more to TOTO)UBLE than meets the eyes (No, they're NOT Transformers). Being overly literal myself, I totally relate to many of)'s comic misunderstandings.

l, I'll admit it—I love dumb s! I hope you do too! ecially since there's even e TOTO TROUBLE to come! ning soon: #3 "The Ace of ers." You don't want to miss bad boy!

Thanks,

Jim

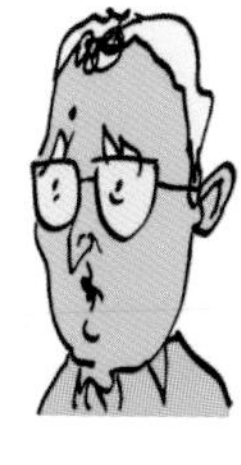

STAY IN TOUCH!

EMAIL: salicrup@papercutz.com
WEB: papercutz.com
TWITTER: @papercutzgn
FACEBOOK: PAPERCUTZGRAPHICNOVELS
MAIL: Papercutz, 160 Broadway, Suite 700,
East Wing, New York, NY 10038

More Great Graphic Novels from PAPERCUTZ

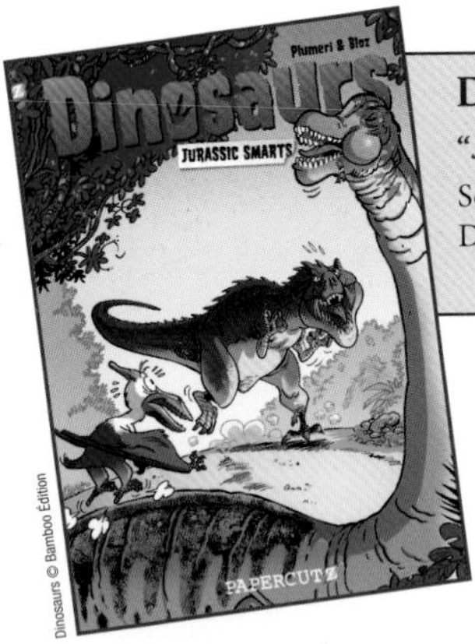
Plumeri & Bloz
Dinosaurs
JURASSIC SMARTS
PAPERCUTZ

DINOSAURS #3
"Jurassic Smarts"
Science facts combined with Dino-humor!

ERNEST & REBECCA #5
"The School of Nonsense"
A 6 ½ year old girl and her microbial buddy against the world!

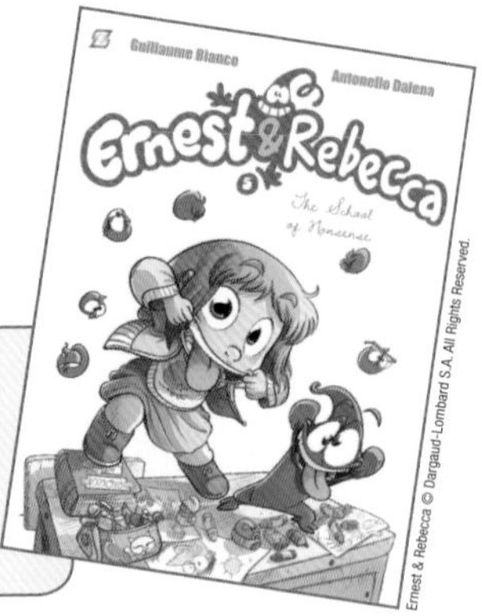
Guillaume Bianco
Antonello Dalena
Ernest & Rebecca
The School of Nonsense

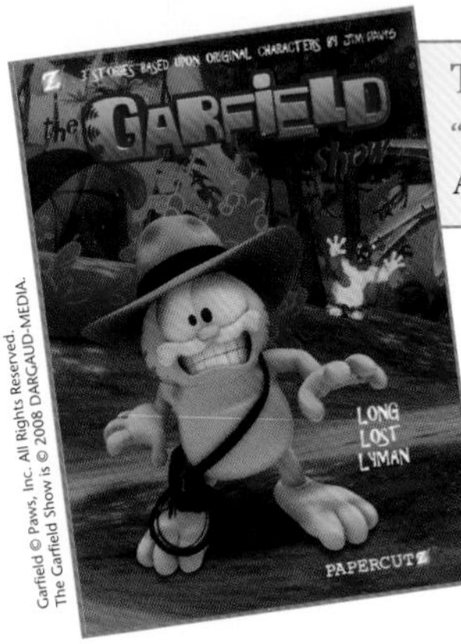
3 STORIES BASED UPON ORIGINAL CHARACTERS BY JIM DAVIS
the GARFIELD Show
LONG LOST LYMAN
PAPERCUTZ

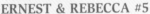

THE GARFIELD SHOW #3
"Long Lost Lyman"
As seen on the Cartoon Network!

BENNY BREAKIRON #4
"Uncle Placid"
Benny helps his Uncle protect the finance minister of Fürengrootsbadenschtein from all kinds of dangerous danger!

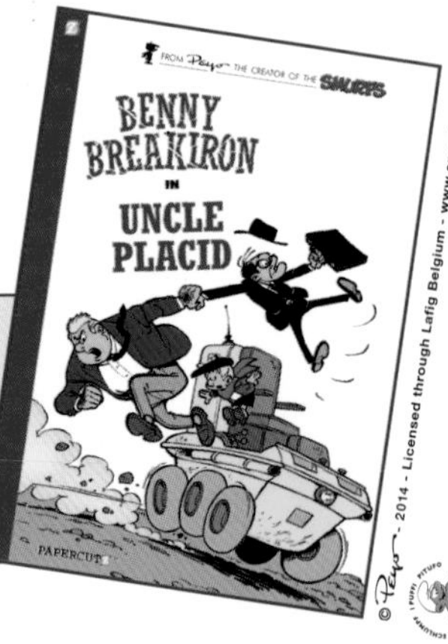
FROM Peyo THE CREATOR OF THE SMURFS
BENNY BREAKIRON
IN
UNCLE PLACID
PAPERCUTZ

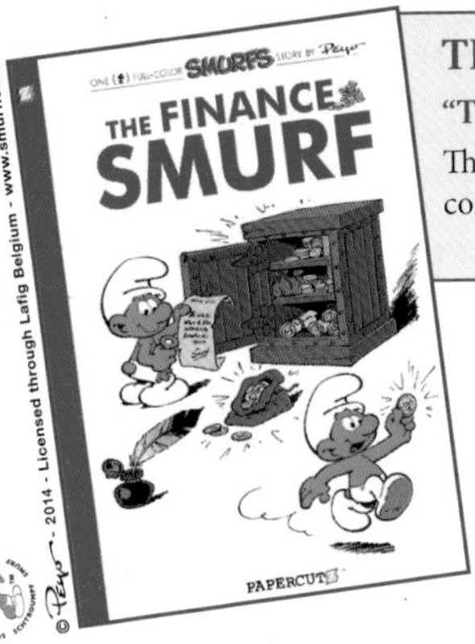
SMURFS
THE FINANCE SMURF
PAPERCUTZ

THE SMURFS #18
"The Finance Smurf"
The Smurfs learn that with money comes problems!

LEGO® NINJAGO #9
"Night of the Nindroids"
Will Zane betray his friends? Plus, an all-new Green Ninja Story!

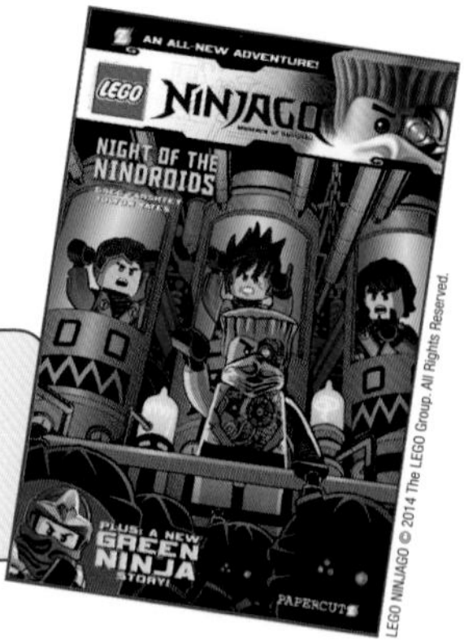
AN ALL-NEW ADVENTURE!
LEGO NINJAGO
NIGHT OF THE NINDROIDS
PLUS A NEW GREEN NINJA STORY!
PAPERCUTZ

Available at better booksellers everywhere!

Or order directly from us! DINOSAURS is available in hardcover only for $10.99; ERNEST & REBECCA is $11.99 in hardcover only; THE GARFIELD SHOW is available in paperback for $7.99, in hardcover for $11.99; BENNY BREAKIRON is available in hardcover only for $11.99; THE SMURFS are available in paperback for $5.99, in hardcover for $10.99; and LEGO NINJAGO is available in paperback for $6.99 and hardcover for $10.99.

Please add $4.00 for postage and handling for the first book, add $1.00 for each additional book.

Please make check payable to NBM Publishing. Send to: PAPERCUTZ, 160 Broadway, Suite 700, East Wing, New York, NY 10038 (1-800-886-1223)